WITH PLAYERS LIKE THESE, THE GAME IS ALWAYS DEADLY

—John and Mary Johnson can't live without each other . . . at least not until each takes a secret lover. The question then becomes: Can they die without each other in "Killed by Kindness"?

—Fargo Scott has a keen eye for larceny but a tin ear for danger when he slips up in "You Can't Be Too Careful."

—Fatstuff is game when Bertha suggests murder, but he winds up the heavy in "Weighty Problem."

—For a smart lawyer, Harold Bannister makes the one move he shouldn't in "Captive Audience."

—The turnover at Mrs. Flynn's boardinghouse is of grave concern to her tenants in "Room to Let."

ALFRED HITCHCOCK'S

GAMES KILLERS PLAY

SEVERN HOUSE

This first UK edition published 1983 by
SEVERN HOUSE PUBLISHERS LTD of
4 Brook Street, London W1Y 1AA

ISBN 0 7278 0930 X

Printed in Great Britain by The Anchor Press Ltd
and bound by Wm Brendon & Son Ltd
both of Tiptree, Essex

ACKNOWLEDGMENTS

"The China Cottage" by August Derleth. Copyright © 1965 by H.S.D. Publications, Inc. Reprinted by permission of the author and the author's agents, Scott Meredith Literary Agency, Inc.

"Killed by Kindness" by Nedra Tyre. Copyright © 1963 by H.S.D. Publications, Inc. Reprinted by permission of the author and the author's agents, Scott Meredith Literary Agency, Inc.

"You Can't Be too Careful" by James Holding. Copyright © 1961 by H.S.D. Publications, Inc. Reprinted by permission of the author and the author's agents, Scott Meredith Literary Agency, Inc.

"Murder Delayed" by Henry Slesar. Copyright © 1962 by H.S.D. Publications, Inc. Reprinted by permission of the author and the author's agents, Theron Raines Literary Agency, Inc.

"Pattern of Guilt" by Helen Nielsen. Copyright © 1958 by H.S.D. Publications, Inc. Reprinted by permission of the author and the author's agents, Scott Meredith Literary Agency, Inc.

"Weighty Problem" by Duane Decker. Copyright © 1960 by H.S.D. Publications, Inc. Reprinted by permission of the author and the author's agents, Scott Meredith Literary Agency, Inc.

"Willie Betts, Banker" by Mike Brett. Copyright © 1965 by H.S.D. Publications, Inc. Reprinted by permission of the author and the author's agents, Scott Meredith Literary Agency, Inc.

"Bus to Chattanooga" by Jonathan Craig. Copyright © 1964 by H.S.D. Publications, Inc. Reprinted by permission of the author and the author's agents, Scott Meredith Literary Agency, Inc.

CONTENTS

INTRODUCTION

I have just spent a pleasant hour leafing through a book devoted to the Acadamy Awards and to the films which have won the Awards through the years. Great films, all of them —though I'll admit to you privately that I often feel that the people who do the voting show real narrowness and limitation of taste by seeming to overlook certain superior suspense films year after year.

In fact, if there is a consistent fault to be found with the films selected for Academy Awards ever since the Academy of Motion Picture Arts and Sciences began its presentations back in 1928, it is that the pictures selected are always so mild, so bland, so tame. I refer particularly to their endings. Look over the list of Academy Award winners from the first one, *Wings,* to the most recent, and you'll find that the endings just—well, end, and limply at that. There isn't a really strong surprise or twist ending among them, as there would have been if they'd just once been sensible enough to select— well, never mind about *that.*

To show you what I mean, I have prepared several examples of the way some of the most famous Academy Award films might have achieved real strength and impact if only their writers and directors had happened to think of these things. Here we go:

1. *Gone with the Wind.* You remember this one, I'm sure. Rhett Butler has found out the kind of person Scarlett really is and is preparing to leave her, and she asks him frantically what will become of her. "Frankly, my dear," says Rhett, "I don't give a damn."

And that, you will recall, is that—curtains down, lights up, and the audience on its way out of the theatre and yawning. No surprise; no shock; just "Frankly, my dear, I don't give a damn." Think how much more shock value there would be if the film ended *this* way:

"Frankly, my dear," says Rhett, "I don't give a damn."

There is a moment's stunned silence. Then Scarlett says, "You can't use that kind of language to a flower of Southern womanhood!" And, seizing a gun from a nearby table, she shoots him through the head, killing him instantly.

2. Or take *Gigi,* which ends with Louis Jourdan realizing that Gigi, played by Leslie Caron, is delightful and that he is falling in love with her. Not much surprise there, you'll have to admit, as everyone seeing the picture knew from the beginning that that was going to happen. But think how much better the picture would have been if there had been a surprise ending caused by the revelation of something else that Jourdan did not realize: *Gigi is really a secret government agent, and the picture ends with her arresting Jourdan for counterfeiting!* (That scene would also explain how Jourdan manages to have so much money to spend throughout the picture without ever working.)

3. *West Side Story* comes closest to achieving the proper kind of surprise ending, for the hero is killed at the end, and only people who've seen or read *Romeo and Juliet* would know that that was coming. And how many are there of those? But you'll have to agree that the ending would have been much more effective *this* way:

The heroine lies sobbing over the hero's limp body. And then suddenly the hero looks up at her, his eyes glazed with death. *"You* got me into this, you louse," he says—and he shoots her, too.

I think you get the general idea. And so, having made my point, I turn you now over to the stories in this collection, whose endings need no changes at all.

—ALFRED HITCHCOCK

THE CHINA COTTAGE

by August Derleth

"My esteemed brother," said Solar Pons as I walked into our quarters one autumn morning for breakfast, "has a mind several times more perceptive than my own, but he has little patience with the processes of ratiocination. Though there is nothing to indicate it, it was certainly he who sent this packet of papers by special messenger well before you were awake."

He had pushed the breakfast dishes back, having barely touched the food Mrs. Johnson had prepared, and sat studying several pages of manuscript, beside which lay an ordinary calling card bearing the name Randolph Curwen, through which someone had scrawled an imperative question mark in red ink.

Observing the direction of my gaze, Pons went on. "The card was clipped to the papers. Curwen is, or perhaps I had better say 'was,' an expert on foreign affairs, and was known to be a consultant of the Foreign Office in cryptology. He was sixty-nine, a widower, and lived alone in Cadogan Place, Belgravia, little given to social affairs since the death of his wife nine years ago. There were no children, but he had the reputation of possessing a considerable estate."

"Is he dead, then?" I asked.

"I should not be surprised to learn that he is," said Pons. "I have had a look at the morning papers, but there is no word of him there. Some important discovery about Curwen has been made. These papers are photographs of some confidential correspondence between members of the German Foreign Office and that of Russia. They would appear to be singularly innocuous, and were probably sent to Curwen so he might examine them for any code."

"I assumed," said an icy voice from the threshold behind me, "that you would have come to the proper conclusion about this data. I came as soon as I could."

Bancroft Pons had come noiselessly into the room, which was no mean feat in view of his weight. His keen eyes were fixed unswervingly upon Pons, his austere face frozen into an impassive mask, which added to the impressiveness of his appearance.

"Sir Randolph?" asked Pons.

"Dead," said Bancroft. "We do not yet know how."

"The papers?"

"We have some reason to believe that a *rapprochement* between Germany and Russia is in the wind. We are naturally anxious to know what impends. We had recourse to Curwen, as one of the most skilled of our cryptologists. He was sent the papers by messenger at noon yesterday."

"I take it he was given the originals."

Bancroft nodded curtly. "Curwen always liked to work with the originals. You've had a chance to look them over."

"They do not seem to be in code," said Pons. "They appear to be only friendly correspondence between the Foreign Secretaries, though it is evident that some increase in trade is being contemplated."

"Curwen was to have telephoned me early this morning. When seven o'clock passed without a call from him, I put in a call. I could not get a reply. So we sent Danvers out. The house and the study were locked. Of course, Danvers had skeleton keys which enabled him to get in. He found Curwen dead in his chair at the table, the papers before him. The windows were all locked, though one was open to a locked screen. Danvers thought he detected a chemical odor of some kind; it suggested that someone might have photographed the papers. But you shall see Curwen. Nothing has been touched. I have a car below. It isn't far to Cadogan Place."

The house in Cadogan Place was austere in its appointments. It was now under heavy police guard; a constable stood on the street before the house, another at the door, and yet another at the door of the study, which was situated at one corner of the front of the house, one pair of windows looking out toward the street, the other into shrubbery-grown grounds to a low stone wall which separated the building from the adjacent property. The house was Georgian in architecture, and likewise in its furniture.

When the study door was unlocked, it revealed book-lined

walls, the shelving broken only by windows and a fireplace.
The walls framed what we had come to see—the great table
in the center of the room, the still-lit lamp, the motionless
form of Sir Randolph Curwen, collapsed in his armchair,
arms dangling floorward, his head thrown back, his face
twisted into an expression of agony. Beside him stood, as if
also on guard, a man whom Bancroft Pons introduced as
Hilary Danvers.

"Nothing has been disturbed, sir."

Bancroft nodded curtly and waved one arm toward the
body. "Sir Randolph, Parker. Your division."

I went around immediately to examine the body. Sir Randolph had been a thin, almost gangling man. A gray mous-
tache decorated his upper lip, and thin gray hair barely con-
cealed his scalp. Pince-nez, one eyeglass broken, dangled from
a black silk cord around his neck. He appeared to have died
in convulsive agony, but there was certainly no visible wound
on his body.

"Heart?" asked Pons.

When I shook my head, he left me to my examination and
walked catlike around the room. He examined the windows,
one after the other, tested the screen on the half-opened window to the grounds, and came to a pause at the fireplace,
where he dropped to one knee.

"Something has been burned here," he said. "Part of the
original material?"

Bancroft said peevishly, "A cursory examination suggests
that someone burned papers with figures on them, as you
can see. We'll collect the ashes and study them, never fear."

Pons rose and came around to the table. He stood to scruti-
nize it, touching nothing. Most of its top was spread with the
papers from the Foreign Office; these were divided into two
piles, with one sheet between them, this one evidently being
the paper Curwen was reading when he was stricken. A pad
of notepaper, free of any jottings, was at one side of this paper. The perimeter of the desk was covered by an assortment
of items ending with a small white, rose-decorated cottage
of china, with an open box of incense pastilles beside it.
Curwen's chair had been pushed slightly back from the table
and around to one side, as if he were making an attempt to
rise before death overtook him.

"Well, Parker?" asked Pons impatiently.

"A seizure of some kind," I replied. "But I fear that only

an autopsy can determine the cause of death precisely. If I had to guess, I'd say poison."

Pons flashed a glance at his brother. "You mentioned an odor on entrance."

"We believe the odor emanated from the incense burner," Mr. Danvers said.

"Ah, this," said Pons, his hand hovering over the china cottage. He gazed inquiringly at Danvers.

"We have tested for fingerprints, Mr. Pons. Only Sir Randolph's were found."

Pons lifted the cottage from its base, where, in a little cup, lay the remains of burned pastilles. He bent his face toward the cup and sniffed. He looked up with narrowed eyes, picked up the base of the china cottage, and thrust it at me.

"What kind of scent might that be, Parker?"

I followed his example and sniffed. "Almond," I said. They make these pastilles in all manner of scents."

Pons put the china cottage back together and picked up the box of pastilles. "Lilac," he said dryly.

"The room was locked, Mr. Pons," put in Danvers. "No one could possibly have got in, if you're suggesting that someone came and poisoned Sir Randolph."

"Child's play," muttered Bancroft impatiently. "What did he find in the papers that someone should want to kill him? Or burn his findings?"

"You're irritable today," said Pons. "There's nothing here to show that Curwen found anything in the papers."

"On the contrary, there is everything to suggest that somehow someone managed entrance into this room, killed Sir Randolph, and burned his notes."

"Why not take them along? If he were clever enough to enter and leave a locked room without a sign to betray him, he must certainly have known that something could be determined from the ashes. I believe the papers in the grate were burned by Sir Randolph himself. He tore off what was on his pad and what had accumulated in his wastebasket under the table, emptied the wastebasket into the fireplace, and set fire to the contents. The ashes are substantial. There is among them at least a page or two from the *Times,* no reason for burning which I could adduce on the part of a foreign agent. Yours is the Foreign Office approach, all intrigue and espionage."

"It is indeed," said Bancroft shortly.

Pons turned again to the china cottage. "If I may, I should like to take this back to Praed Street." He picked up also the box of pastilles. "And this."

Bancroft stared at him as if he were convinced that Pons had taken leave of his senses.

"This is bone china," Pons said, with a hint of a smile at his lips. "Of Staffordshire origin, it dates, I should say, to the early nineteenth century. This china, though translucent, will tolerate a surprising amount of heat."

"Pray spare me this lecture," said Bancroft icily. "Take it."

Pons thanked him dryly, slipped the box of pastilles into his pocket, and handed the china cottage to me. "Handle it with care, Parker. We shall examine it at our leisure at 7B." He turned again to his brother. "Sir Randolph lived alone. Surely there were servants?"

"A Mrs. Claudia Melton came in to clean the house twice a week," said Bancroft. "And there was a man-servant by day, Will Davinson. He prepared Sir Randolph's meals and tended to the door. He has come in, if you wish to question him. If so, let us get about it at once."

Bancroft signaled to the constable who stood at the threshold, and he led us out of the room to the rear quarters. In a combination kitchen and breakfast room, there sat waiting a middle-aged man who, immediately on our entrance, clicked his heels together, standing like a ramrod.

"Mr. Davinson," said the constable, "Mr. Solar Pons would like to ask you some questions."

"At your service, sir."

"Pray sit down, Mr. Davinson."

Davinson regained his chair and sat waiting expectantly. His eyes were alert and conveyed the impression of youth the rest of his body belied.

"You were Sir Randolph's orderly in the war?" asked Pons abruptly.

"Yes, sir."

"You had reason then to know his habits very well?"

"Yes, sir."

"He seems to have been addicted to the burning of incense."

"He has burned it for as long as I've known him."

"You will have had occasion to ascertain how many pastilles a day he customarily burned."

"Sir, he released the fragrant smoke only when he retired

to his study. This was usually in the evening. He seldom
burned more than three in an evening, and commonly but
two."

"His favorite scent?"

"Lilac. But he also had pastilles scented with rose, almond,
thyme, and, I believe, lavender. He always had a good sup-
ply."

Pons took a turn down the room and back. He stood for
a few moments in silence, his eyes closed, his right hand pulling at his earlobe.

"Sir Randolph was a reclusive man?"

"He saw very few people."

"Whom did he see in the past fortnight?"

Davinson concentrated for a moment. "His niece, Miss
Emily Curwen. She had come to London from her home in
Edinburgh and came to call. That was perhaps a trifle over
two weeks ago."

"No matter," said Pons. "Go on."

"Mr. Leonard Loveson of Loveson & Fitch in High Hol-
born. That was a business matter. Sir Randolph held a mortgage on their place of business."

"Sir Randolph held other such mortgages?"

"I was not in Sir Randolph's confidence, sir, but I believe
he did."

"Go on, Mr. Davinson."

"Well, then there was a great-nephew, Ronald Lindall, the
son of Miss Emily's sister, also from Edinburgh; he was at
the house six days ago, paying a courtesy visit, I took it."

"Anyone else?"

"Yes," said Davinson hesitantly. "There was a legal gentleman two days ago, all fuss and feathers. They had words,
but briefly. Sir Randolph soothed him and sent him off. I
believe the matter concerned another of Sir Randolph's mortgages."

"He was a hard man?"

"No, sir. Quite the contrary. More than once he remitted
interest due him—even cancelled it. And on one occasion
he forgave a small mortgage. No, sir, he was far too easy a
man to deal with. Some of them took advantage of him."

Pons took another turn around the room. "Of these people,
which were familiar visitors?" he asked.

"Mr. Loveson."

"You had not seen Miss Emily before?"

"No, sir. Sir Randolph had spoken of her, but she had not visited at any time that I was in this house."

"You admitted her?"

"Yes, sir. Sir Randolph never answered the door. If I had gone, unless he had an appointment, he did not answer the door at all."

"Will you cast your mind back to Miss Emily's visit? How did she seem to you?"

"I don't follow you, Mr. Pons."

"Was she composed—sad, gay, what?"

"She seemed to be a trifle agitated, if I may say so. But that was when she left, Mr. Pons. When she came in she was very much a lady."

"She and her uncle had words?"

"I could not say." Davinson was suddenly prim.

"Mr. Lindall, now."

"He was a somewhat truculent young man, but apologetic about disturbing Sir Randolph. They had a pleasant visit. Sir Randolph showed him about the house and garden, and he took his leave."

"Mr. Loveson. Do you know, is the mortgage a large one, presuming it has not been settled?"

"I don't know, but I had the impression that it is quite large." Davinson swallowed and cleared his throat. "I must emphasize again, Mr. Pons, that while Sir Randolph did not take me into his confidence, I was able to come to certain conclusions about his affairs."

"One could hardly expect otherwise of a companion of such long standing."

Davinson inclined his head slightly as if modestly accepting faint praise.

"The gentlemen from the Foreign Office," Pons said then. "Did you admit them?"

"No, sir. They came after I had gone to my flat."

"You answered the telephone while you were here. Do you recall any appointments after your hours during the past two weeks?"

"The foreign gentleman, three nights ago."

"Did he leave his name?"

"No, sir. He asked to speak with Sir Randolph. He spoke in a German accent. Sir Randolph was in his study. I made the signal with the buzzer, and Sir Randolph took the call.

I stayed on the wire just long enough to be sure the connection had been made."

"You heard their conversation?"

"Sir, only enough to know that Sir Randolph was very much surprised—I took it, agreeably. Afterward, he came out and instructed me to prepare some sandwiches and chill some wine. So I knew he expected someone to come in during the evening. I assumed it was the foreign gentleman."

Pons nodded. "Your living arrangements were by your choice, Mr. Davinson?"

"No, sir. That was the way Sir Randolph wished it. He never wanted to be valeted, didn't like it. But he needed someone to do the ordinary things in the house during the day."

"You have your own keys?"

"Yes, Mr. Pons."

"Sir Randolph was secretive?"

"Only about his work. He was a gentleman who, I should say, preferred his own company to that of anyone else. He treated me very well. Indeed, if I may say so, I should not be surprised to find myself mentioned in his will. He hinted as much to me on several occasions, and that ought to be proof enough that he was not unnecessarily secretive."

"Thank you, Mr. Davinson. I may call on you again."

"I want to do anything I can to help, sir. I was very fond of Sir Randolph. We were, if I may say so, almost like stepbrothers."

"Was that not an odd way of putting it?" asked Bancroft, when we were walking away from the kitchen. "One says, 'We were like brothers.' Stepbrothers, indeed!"

"Probably not, for Davinson," said Pons. "I fancy it was his way of saying they were like brothers one step removed on the social scale, Sir Randolph being a step up, and he a step down."

Bancroft grunted explosively. "You've frittered away half an hour. To what conclusions have you come?"

"I daresay it's a trifle early to be certain of very much. I submit, however, that Sir Randolph was murdered by someone he had no reason to fear. He appears to have been a cautious man, one not given to carelessness in the matter of his relationship with the public."

"You have some ingenious theory about the murderer's

entrance into and exit from the locked room, no doubt," said Bancroft testily.

"I should hardly call it that. Sir Randolph admitted him, and Sir Randolph saw him out, locking the doors after him. Until we have the autopsy report, we cannot know precisely how Sir Randolph was done to death."

"We are having the papers gone over once again."

"A waste of time. You Foreign Office people think in painfully conventional patterns. I submit the papers have nothing to do with it."

Bancroft protested, "Surely it is too much to believe that Sir Randolph's possession of these papers at the time of his death amounts only to coincidence?"

"It is indeed an outrageous coincidence," said Pons. "But I am forced to believe it."

"Is there anything more here?" asked Bancroft.

"If possible, I should like to have a copy of Sir Randolph's will sent to 7B without delay."

"It will be done."

Back at our quarters, Pons retired with the china cottage and the box of pastilles to the corner where he kept his chemicals, while I prepared to go out on my round. When I left 7B, he was in the process of breaking apart one of the scented pastilles; when I returned two hours later, he had broken them all apart and was just rising from his examination, his eyes dancing with the light of discovery.

"Sir Randolph came to his death by his own hand."

"Suicide!"

"I have not said so. No, one of the pastilles contained cyanide. It was prepared and placed among the pastilles in the box on the desk, unknown to him. Since he used not less than two pastilles a day and not more than three, and the box contains normally two dozen pastilles, we can assume the poisoned pastille was placed there not more than twelve days ago. From the ashes in the china cottage it is possible to determine that the cyanide was enclosed in inflammable wax, and this enclosed in the customary formula. Sir Randolph fell victim to a death trap which had been laid for him by someone who both knew his habits and had access to his study."

"I thought it poison. What was the motive?"

"It was certainly not the papers, as was evident the moment I concluded that the incense burner was the source of Sir Randolph's death. That faint odor of almond, you will remember, was indicative."

"His estate then?"

"We shall see. Only a few minutes before your return a copy of Sir Randolph's will arrived. I was about to examine it."

He crossed to the table, took up the sealed envelope lying there, and opened it. He stood for a few moments studying the paper he unfolded. "An admirably clear document," he murmured. "To his faithful servant, Will Davinson, twenty-five hundred pounds. To Miss Emily, 'who is otherwise provided for,' the sum of five hundred pounds. To Mrs. Claudia Melton, two hundred pounds. The bulk of his estate distributed equally among five charitable institutions. All mortgages forgiven!"

"There is certainly not much in the way of motive there," I said.

"Murder has been committed for as much as ten pounds," said Pons. "And less. But hardly with such care and premeditation. I fancy the stake was considerably more than two or five hundred pounds."

"Davinson has motive and opportunity."

"He could hardly deny it," observed Pons with a crooked smile.

"He knew he was mentioned in the will. He told us as much."

"Rack up one point against his having planned Sir Randolph's death."

"I recall your saying often that when all the impossible solutions have been eliminated, then whatever remains, however improbable, must be the truth." Parker continued, "Davinson spoke of a foreigner, a German, who visited Sir Randolph only a few days before his death."

"We have only Davinson's word for it," said Pons.

"If not the papers from the Foreign Office, we seem to be left with only Sir Randolph's estate for motive," I pointed out, with some asperity.

"His estate seems to be well accounted for."

"The mortgage holders!" I cried.

"I have thought of them. Even before I saw this document, I suggested that some inquiry be set afoot about them. But I venture to predict it will be disclosed that Sir Randolph did not hold many unpaid mortgages, and that the total sum involved is not as large as Davinson, for one, believed."

"The man Loveson?"

"I have not forgotten him. His will very probably turn out to be the largest outstanding mortgage. He may have had motive in addition to having opportunity. The probability, again, is remote, for it must surely have occurred to him, should any thought of killing Sir Randolph have crossed his mind, that his motive would be instantly perceived. Moreover, we have Davinson's word for Sir Randolph's lenience with his debtors, and this is given adequate support by the terms of Sir Randolph's will, forgiving his mortgages. No, there is something else here of which we have as yet no inkling, something that induced his murderer to go to great pains to prepare a deadly pastille, secrete it among those on the table during the time of his visit with Sir Randolph—or his secret entry into the house, if it were that—and then be safely away when his victim by chance selected the poisoned pastille for use. It was all very carefully premeditated; there was nothing impulsive about it. That is why, patently, the papers have nothing to do with the matter, for whoever put the pastille into the box did so well before even Sir Randolph knew that he would be sent the papers for examination. By the same process of deduction, the foreign visitor lacked motive—if there were such a visitor."

"And if not?"

"Then, I fear, we should have to put Davinson through it. But there is little reason to doubt Davinson's story. A foreign visitor to Sir Randolph is not unlikely. And Davinson does not seem to me to be capable of so elaborate a plan."

"Who then?"

"We must consider that Davinson was gone by night. Sir Randolph was alone. He could have given entry to anyone he pleased, regardless of what Davinson believes."

"Well, then, we get back to motive."

"Do we not?" So saying, Pons sank into a reverie, from which he stirred only to eat, with a preoccupied air, a lunch Mrs. Johnson sent up. He still sat, smoking pipe after pipe of his abominable shag, when at last I went to bed.

Pons' hand at my shoulder woke me while it was yet dark.

"Can you spare the day, Parker?" he asked, when I sat up. "We have just time to catch the four o'clock from King's Cross for Edinburgh."

"Edinburgh?" I queried, getting out of bed.

"I have an unyielding fancy to learn what the late Sir Randolph and his niece had words about. We lose a day by traveling later. The four o'clock brings us into Edinburgh by one-thirty this afternoon. We shall have ample opportunity to make our enquiries of Miss Emily Curwen. You will have hours to sleep on the train."

"Miss Emily!" I cried. "For five hundred pounds? Preposterous!"

"Unlikely, perhaps, but hardly preposterous," retorted Pons. "Poison, after all, is primarily a woman's weapon so she is a suspect."

Pons had already summoned a cab, which waited below. As soon as I had dressed and made arrangements for my locum tenens to call on my patients for the next two days, we were off for King's Cross station, which we reached just in time to catch the train for Scotland.

Once in our compartment and northward bound out of London, Pons sank again into cogitation, and I settled myself to resume the sleep Pons had interrupted.

When I woke in the late morning hours, Pons sat watching the lovely countryside flow by. We had crossed the Scottish border, and soon the familiar heights of Arthur's Seat, the Salisbury Crags, the Braid Hills and Corstorphine Hill would come into view. Here and there little pockets of ground mist still held to the hollows, but the sun shone, and the day promised to be fine.

The tranquil expression of Pons' face told me nothing.

"You cannot have been serious in suggesting that Miss Curwen poisoned her uncle," I said.

"I am not yet in a position to make that suggestion," replied Pons, turning away from the pane. "However, a curious chain of events offers itself for our consideration. There is nothing to show that Miss Emily visited her uncle at any time previous to her recent visit. Then she comes, they have words, she hurries off, distraught. Does not this suggest anything to you?"

"Obviously they quarreled."

"But what about? Two people who have not seen each other for many years, as far as we know, can hardly, on such short notice, have much to quarrel about."

"Unless there is a matter of long standing between them."

"Capital! Capital, Parker," said Pons, his eyes twinkling. "But what ancient disagreement could exist between uncle and niece?"

"A family estrangement?"

"There is always that possibility," conceded Pons. "However, Miss Emily would hardly have come, in that case, unannounced and without an invitation to do so."

"Perhaps, unknown to Davinson, she had been invited to come," I said.

"Perhaps. I am inclined to doubt it. Miss Emily yielded to the impulse to confront her uncle to ask some favor of him. His failure to grant it angered her and she rushed off."

"That is hardly consistent with the premeditation so evident in the careful preparation of a poisoned pastille," I couldn't help pointing out. As usual, it was superfluous.

"Granted, Parker. But there's nothing to prevent such premeditation in the event that the favor she asked her uncle were not granted."

"What could it have been that, failing its granting, only his death would serve her?" I protested. "If a matter of long standing, then, why not longer? No, Pons, it won't wash, it won't at all. I fear you have allowed your latent distrust of the sex to darken your view of Miss Emily Curwen."

Pons burst into hearty laughter.

"Where are we bound for? Do you know?"

"Miss Emily lives in her father's house on Northumberland Street, in the New Town. I took time yesterday to ascertain this and other facts. She and her sister were the only children of Sir Randolph's brother, Andrew. Her sister married unwisely, a man who squandered her considerable inheritance. Both the elder Lindalls are now dead, survived by an only son, Ronald, who is employed in a bookshop on Torphichen Street. But here we are, drawing into Edinburgh."

Within the hour we stood on the stoop of the house on Northumberland Street. Pons rang the bell three times before the door was opened, only a little, and an inquiring face looked out at us there.

"Miss Emily Curwen?"

"Yes?"

"Mr. Solar Pons, of London, at your service. Dr. Parker and I have come about the matter of your uncle's death."

There was a moment of pungent silence. Then the door was opened wide, and Miss Curwen stood there, unmistakably shocked and surprised. "Uncle Randolph dead? I saw him within the month. The picture of health!" she cried. "But forgive me. Come in, gentlemen, do."

Miss Emily led the way to the drawing room of the old-fashioned house, which was certainly at one time the abode of wealth. She was a woman approaching fifty, with a good figure still, and betraying some evidence in the care she had taken with her chestnut hair and her cosmetics of trying to retain as much of a youthful aspect as possible.

"Pray sit down," she said. "Tell me of uncle's death. What happened? Was it an accident?"

"Perhaps, in a manner of speaking, it was," said Pons. "He was found dead in his study."

"Poor uncle!" she cried, unaffectedly.

She seemed unable to fix her eyes on either Pons or myself. Her hands were busy plucking at her dress, or lacing her fingers together, or carrying her fingers to her lips.

"Perhaps you did not know he left you five hundred pounds?"

"No, I did not." Then her eyes brightened quite suddenly. "Poor, dear uncle! He needn't have done that. Now that he's gone, I shall have it all! All!"

"Somewhat over a fortnight ago you called on your uncle, Miss Curwen."

"Yes, I did." She grimaced.

"You found him well at that time?"

"I believe I have said as much, sir."

"You left him, upset. Was he unkind to you?"

"Sir, it was the old matter. Now it is resolved."

"Would you care to tell us about it?"

"Oh, there's no secret in it, I assure you. Everyone knows of it here in Edinburgh." She tossed her head and shrugged, pitying herself briefly. "Uncle Randolph was as hard a man as my father. My older sister, Cicely, made a very bad marriage in our father's eyes. He had settled her inheritance on her, and when he saw how Arthur wasted it, he made certain I could never do the same. So he put my inheritance, fifty thousand pounds, in trust, and made Uncle Randolph guardian of the trust. I could have only so much a year to live on, a pittance. But the world has changed, and everyone knows that it is not so easy to live on a restricted income as it was twenty-five years ago when my father died. But now all that's over. Now that Uncle Randolph's dead, what is mine comes to me free of his or anyone's control."

"You must have had assistance, Miss Curwen," said Pons sympathetically.

"Oh, yes. My nephew, my dear boy! He's all I have, gentlemen. He has cared for his old aunt quite as if I were his own mother. I've been very much alone here. What could I do, what society could I have, on so limited an income? Now all that is changed. I am sorry Uncle Randolph is dead, but I'm not sorry the restrictions on my inheritance are removed."

Pons' glance flickered about the room, which looked as if it had not quite emerged into the twentieth century. "A lovely room, Miss Curwen," he observed.

"My grandfather planned it. I hate it," she said simply. "I shall lose no time selling the house. Think of having fifty thousand pounds I might have had when I was in my twenties! Oh, Mr. Pons, how cruel it was! My father thought I'd do the same thing my sister did, even after I saw how it went with them."

"I see you, too, are given to the use of incense, Miss Curwen," said Pons, his gaze fastened to a china castle.

"Any scent will serve to diminish the mould and mildew, gentlemen."

"May I look at that incense burner?" persisted Pons.

"Please do."

Pons crossed to the mantel where the china castle rested, picked it up, and brought it back to his chair. It was an elaborate creation in bone china, featuring three lichen-covered turrets, and evidently three burners. Carnations adorned it, and a vine of green leaves, and morning glories. Its windows were outlined in soft brown.

"A Colebrook Dale marking on this Coalport castle identifies it as prior to 1850 in origin," said Pons.

Miss Curwen's eyebrows went up. "You're a collector, sir?"

"Only of life's oddities," said Pons. "But I have some interest in antiquities as well." He looked up. "And what scent do you favor, Miss Curwen?"

"Rose."

"One could have guessed that you would select so complimentary a fragrance, Miss Curwen."

Miss Curwen blushed prettily as Pons got up to return the

china castle to the mantel, where he stood for a few moments with the opened box of pastilles in his hand, inhaling deeply the scent that emanated from it. He appeared to have some difficulty closing the box before he turned once more and came back to where he had been sitting. He did not sit down again.

"I fear we have imposed upon you long enough, Miss Curwen," said Pons.

Miss Emily came to her feet. "I suppose you will take care of such legalities as there are, gentlemen?"

"I fancy Sir Randolph's legal representatives will do that in good time, Miss Curwen," said Pons.

"Oh! I thought . . ."

"I am sorry to have given you the wrong impression. I am a private enquiry agent, Miss Curwen. There is some question about the manner of your uncle's death; I am endeavoring to answer it."

She was obviously perplexed. "Well, there's nothing I can tell you about that. I know he was in what looked like perfect health when I last saw him."

She did not seem to have the slightest suspicion of Pons' objective, and walked us to the door, where she let us out. From the stoop, we could hear the chain being quietly slid back into place.

"I must hand it to you, Pons," I said. "There's motive for you."

"Poor woman! I'll wager she's dancing around by herself in celebration now," he said as we walked back down to the street. "There are pathetic people in this world to whom the possession of money is everything. They know little of life and nothing of how to live. Presumably Andrew Curwen was such a one; I fear Miss Emily may be another. One could live well on the income of fifty thousand pounds if one had a mind to, but Miss Emily preferred to pine and grieve and feel sorry for herself, a lonely, deluded woman. I shall be sorry to add to her loneliness, but perhaps her wealth will assuage her. But come, Parker, we have little time to lose. We must be off to the police. With luck, we shall be able to catch one of the night trains back to London."

Inspector Brian McGavick joined us when Pons explained his need. He was in plainclothes, and looked considerably more like an actor than a member of the constabulary.

"I've heard about you, Mr. Pons," said McGavick. "This

morning, on instructions from the Foreign Office. I am at your service."

"Inspector, you're in charge here. I have no authority. I shall expect you to take whatever action the events of the next hour or two call for." He outlined briefly the circumstances surrounding the murder of Sir Randolph Curwen. By the time he had finished we had arrived in Torphichen Street.

"Let us just park the car over here," said Pons, "and walk the rest of the way."

We got out of the police car and walked leisurely down the street to a little shop that bore the sign, *Laidlaw's Books*. There Pons turned in.

A stout little man clad almost formally, save for his plaid weskit, came hurrying up to wait on us.

"Just browsing, sir," said Pons.

The little man bowed and returned to resume his place on a stool at a high, old-fashioned desk in a far corner of the shop. The three of us began to examine the books in the stalls and on the shelves, following Pons' lead. Pons soon settled down to a stall containing novels of Sir Walter Scott and Dickens, studying one volume after another with that annoying air of having the entire afternoon in which to do it.

In a quarter of an hour, the door of the shop opened to admit a handsome young man who walked directly back to the rear of the shop, removed his hat and ulster, and came briskly back to attend to us. Since Pons was nearest him, he walked directly up to Pons and engaged him in conversation I could not overhear until I drifted closer.

"There is merit in each," Pons was saying. "Scott for his unparalleled reconstruction of Scotland's past, Dickens for the remarkable range of his characters, however much some of them may seem caricatures. I think of establishing special shelves for each when I open my own shop."

"Ah, you're a bookman, sir? Where?"

"In London. I lack only a partner."

"I would like to be in London myself. What are your qualifications?"

"I need a young man, acquainted with books and authors, capable of putting a little capital into the business. Are you interested?"

"I might be."

Pons thrust forth his hand. "Name's Holmes," he said.

"Lindall," said the young man, taking his hand.

"Capital?" asked Pons.

"I expect to come into some."

"When?"

"Within the next few months."

"Ample time! Now tell me, Mr. Lindall, since I am in need of some other little service, do you know any chemistry? Ever studied it?"

"No, sir."

"I asked because I saw a chemist's shop next door. Perhaps you have a friend there who might make up a special prescription for me?"

"As a matter of fact, I do have. A young man named Ardley. Ask for him and say I gave you his name."

"Thank you, thank you. I am grateful. In delicate little matters like these, one cannot be too careful."

Lindall's interest quickened. He ran the tip of his tongue over his lips and asked, "What is the nature of the prescription, sir?"

Pons dipped his hand into his coat pocket, thrust it out before Lindall, and unfolded his fingers. "I need a little pastille like this—with cyanide at the center, to dispose of old men and middle-aged ladies."

Lindall's reaction was extraordinary. He threw up his hands as if to thrust Pons away, stumbled backward, and upset a stall of books. Books and Lindall together went crashing to the floor.

"Oh, I say! I say now!" called out the proprietor, getting off his stool.

"Inspector McGavick, arrest this man for the murder of Sir Randolph Curwen, and the planned murder of his aunt, Miss Emily Curwen," said Pons.

McGavick had already moved in on Lindall, and was pulling him to his feet.

"You will need this poisoned pastille, Inspector. I found it in a box of rose pastilles in Miss Emily's home. You should have no difficulty proving that this and the one that killed Sir Randolph were manufactured for Lindall at his direction." To Lindall, Pons added, "A pity you didn't ask after my Christian name, Mr. Lindall. Sherlock. A name I assume on those special occasions when I feel inordinately immodest."

In our compartment on the 10:15 express for London Pons answered the questions with which I pelted him.

"It was an elementary matter, Parker," he said, "confused by the coincidence of Sir Randolph's possession of the Foreign Office papers. The death trap had been laid for him well before anyone at all knew that he would see the papers in question. This motive eliminated, it became necessary to disclose another. Nobody appeared to dislike Sir Randolph, and it did not seem that any adequate motivation lay in the provisions of his will.

"We were left, then, with Miss Emily's curious visit, angrily terminated. She went to London to appeal to her uncle for an end to the trust. She came back and complained to her nephew—her 'dear boy' who is 'all' she has—her designated heir, as an examination of her will will certainly show. In a fortnight, familiarized with Sir Randolph's habits by Miss Emily, he paid him a visit on his own, managed to slip the poisoned pastille into his box, and was off to bide his time. He had had two made, one for his aunt, and felt safe in slipping the other into her box of pastilles. He might better have waited, but he had not counted on the death of Sir Randolph being taken for anything but a seizure of some kind. He underestimated the police, I fear, and greed pushed him too fast. 'The love of money,' Parker, is indeed 'the root of all evil.' "

KILLED BY KINDNESS

by Nedra Tyre

John Johnson knew that he must murder his wife. He had to. It was the only decent thing he could do. He owed her that much consideration.

Divorce was out of the question. He had no grounds. Mary was kind and pretty and pleasant company and hadn't ever glanced at another man. Not once in their marriage had she nagged him. She was a marvelous cook and an excellent bridge player. No hostess in town was more popular.

It seemed a pity that he would have to kill her. But he certainly wasn't going to shame her by telling her he was leaving her; not when they'd just celebrated their twentieth anniversary two months before and had congratulated each other on being the happiest married couple in the whole world. With pink champagne, and in front of dozens of admiring friends, they had pledged undying love. They had said they hoped fate would be kind and would allow them to die together. After all that, John couldn't just toss Mary aside. Such a trick would be the action of a cad.

Without him Mary would have no life at all. Of course, she would have her shop, which had done well since she had opened it, but she wasn't a real career woman. Opening the shop had been a kind of lark when the Greer house, next door to them in a row of town houses, had been put up for sale. No renovation or remodeling had been done except to knock down part of a wall so that the two houses could be connected by a door. The furniture shop was only something to occupy her time, Mary said, while her sweet husband worked. It didn't mean anything to her, though she had a good business sense. John seldom went in the shop. Come to think of it, it was a jumble. It made him a little uneasy; everything in it seemed so crowded and precarious.

Yes, Mary's interest was in him; it wasn't in the shop.

She'd have to have something besides the shop to have any meaningful existence.

If he divorced her she'd have no one to take her to concerts and plays. Dinner parties, her favorite recreation, would be out. None of their friends would invite her to come without him. Alone and divorced, she would be shunted into the miserable category of spinsters and widows who had to be invited to lunch instead of dinner.

He couldn't relegate Mary to such a life, though he felt sure that if he asked her for a divorce she'd give him one. She was so acquiescent and accommodating.

No, he wasn't going to humiliate her by asking for a divorce. She deserved something better from him than that.

If only he hadn't met Lettice on that business trip to Lexington. But how could he regret such a miracle? He had come alive only in the six weeks since he'd known Lettice. Life with Mary was ashes in comparison. Since he'd met Lettice he felt like a blind man who had been given sight. He might have been deaf all his life and was hearing for the first time. And the marvel was that Lettice loved him and was eager to marry him, and free to marry him.

And waiting.

And insisting.

He must concentrate on putting Mary out of the way. Surely a little accident could be arranged without too much trouble. The shop ought to be an ideal place, there in all that crowded junk. Among those heavy marble busts and chandeliers and andirons something from above or below could be used to dispatch his dear Mary to her celestial reward.

"Darling, you must tell your wife," Lettice urged when they next met at their favorite hotel in Lexington. "You've got to arrange for a divorce. You have to. You've got to tell her about us." Lettice's voice was so low and musical that John felt hypnotized.

But how could he tell Mary about Lettice?

John couldn't even rationalize Lettice's appeal to himself.

Instead of Mary's graciousness, Lettice had elegance. Lettice wasn't as pretty or as charming as Mary. But he couldn't resist her. In her presence he was an ardent, masterful lover; in Mary's presence he was a thoughtful, complaisant husband. With Lettice life would always be lived at the highest peak; nothing in his long years with Mary could approach the wonder he had known during his few meetings with Lettice. Lettice was earth, air, fire and water, the four elements; Mary was—no, he couldn't compare them. Anyway, what good was it to set their attractions off against each other?

Then, just as he was about to suggest to Lettice that they go to the bar, he saw Chet Fleming enter the hotel and walk across the lobby toward the desk. What was Chet Fleming doing in Lexington? But then anyone could be anywhere. That was the humiliating risk illicit lovers faced. They might be discovered anywhere, anytime. No place was secure for them. But Chet Fleming was the one person he wanted least to see, and the one who would make the most of encountering John with another woman. That blabbermouth would tell his wife and friends, his doctor, his grocer, his banker, his lawyer. Word would get back to Mary. Her heart would be broken. She deserved better than that.

John cowered beside Lettice. Chet dawdled at the desk. John couldn't be exposed like that any longer, a single glance around and Chet would see him and Lettice. John made an incoherent excuse, then sidled over to the newsstand where he hid behind a magazine until Chet had registered and had taken an elevator upstairs.

Anyway, they had escaped, but only barely.

John couldn't risk cheapening their attachment. He had to do something to make it permanent right away, but at the same time he didn't want to hurt Mary.

Thousands of people in the United States had gotten up that morning who would be dead before nightfall. Why couldn't his dear Mary be among them? Why couldn't she die without having to be murdered?

When John rejoined Lettice and tried to explain his panic, she was composed but concerned and emphatic.

"Darling, this incident only proves what I've been insisting. I said you'd have to tell your wife at once. We can't go on like this. Surely you understand."

"Yes, dear, you're quite right. I'll do something as soon as I can."

"You must do something immediately, darling."

Oddly enough, Mary Johnson was in the same predicament as John Johnson. She had had no intention of falling in love. In fact, she thought she was in love with her husband. How naïve she'd been before Kenneth came into her shop that morning asking whether she had a bust of Mozart. Of course, she had a bust of Mozart; she had several busts of Mozart, not to mention Bach, Beethoven, Victor Hugo, Balzac, Shakespeare, George Washington and Goethe, in assorted sizes.

He had introduced himself. Customers didn't ordinarily introduce themselves, and she gave him her name in return, and then realized that he was the outstanding interior designer in town.

"Quite frankly," he said, "I wouldn't be caught dead with this bust of Mozart and it will ruin the room, but my client insists on having it. Do you mind if I see what else you have?"

She showed him all over the shop then. Later she tried to recall the exact moment when they had fallen in love. He had spent all that first morning there; toward noon he seemed especially attracted to a small back room cluttered and crowded with chests of drawers. He reached for a drawer pull that came off in his hands, then he reached for her.

"What do you think you're doing?" she said. "Goodness, suppose some customers come in."

"Let them browse," he said.

She couldn't believe that it had happened, but it had. Afterward, instead of being lonely when John went out of town on occasional business trips, she yearned for the time when he gave her his antiseptic peck of a kiss and told her he would be gone overnight.

The small back room jammed with the chests of drawers became Mary's and Kenneth's discreet rendezvous. They added a chaise longue.

One day a voice reached them there. They had been too engrossed to notice that anyone had approached.

"Mrs. Johnson, where are you? I'd like some service, please."

Mary stumbled out from the dark to greet the customer. Mary tried to smooth her mussed hair. She knew that her lipstick was smeared.

The customer was Mrs. Bryan, the most accomplished gossip in town. Mrs. Bryan would get word around that Mary Johnson was carrying on scandalously in her shop. John was sure to find out now.

Fortunately, Mrs. Bryan was preoccupied. She was in a

Pennsylvania Dutch mood and wanted to see butter molds and dower chests.

It was a lucky escape, as Mary later told Kenneth. Kenneth refused to be reassured.

"I love you deeply," he said. "And honorably. I've reason to know you love me, too. I'm damned tired of sneaking around. I'm not going to put up with it any longer. Do you understand? We've got to get married. Tell your husband you want a divorce."

Kenneth kept talking about a divorce, as if a divorce was nothing at all—no harder to arrange than a dental appointment. How could she divorce a man who had been affectionate and kind and faithful for twenty years? How could she snatch happiness from him?

If only John would die. Why couldn't he have a heart attack? Every day thousands of men died from heart attacks. Why couldn't her darling John just drop dead? It would simplify everything.

Even the ringing of the telephone sounded angry, and when Mary answered it Kenneth, at the other end of the line, was in a rage.

"Damn it, Mary, this afternoon was ridiculous. It was insulting. I'm not skulking any more. I'm not hiding behind doors while you grapple around for butter molds to show customers. We've got to be married right away."

"Yes, darling. Do be patient."

"I've already been too patient. I'm not waiting any longer."

She knew that he meant it. If she lost Kenneth life would end for her. She hadn't ever felt this way about John.

Dear John. How could she toss him aside? He was in the prime of life; he could live decades longer. All his existence was centered on her. He lived to give her pleasure. They had no friends except other married people. John would have to lead a solitary life if she left him. He'd be odd man out without her; their friends would invite him to their homes because they were sorry for him. Poor, miserable John was what everyone would call him. He'd be better off dead, they'd say. He would neglect himself; he wouldn't eat regularly; he would have to live alone in some wretched furnished apartment. No, she mustn't condemn him to an existence like that.

Why had this madness with Kenneth started? Why had that foolish woman insisted on having a bust of Mozart in her music room? Why had Kenneth come to her shop in search of it when busts of Mozart were in every secondhand store on Broad Street and at much cheaper prices?

Yet she wouldn't have changed anything. Seconds with Kenneth were worth lifetimes with John.

Only one end was possible. She would have to think of a nice, quick, efficient, unmessy way to get rid of John.

And soon.

John had never seen Mary look as lovely as she did that night when he got home from his business trip. For one flicker of a second, life with her seemed enough. Then he thought of Lettice, and the thought stunned him into the belief that no act that brought them together could be criminal. He must get on with what he had to do. He must murder Mary in as gentlemanly a way as possible, and he must do it that very night. Meantime he would enjoy the wonderful dinner Mary had prepared for him. Common politeness demanded it, and anyhow he was ravenous.

Yes, he must get on with the murder just as soon as he finished eating. It seemed a little heartless to be contriving a woman's death even as he ate her cheese cake, but he certainly didn't mean to be callous.

He didn't know just how he would murder Mary. Perhaps if he could get her into her shop, there in that corner where all the statuary was, he could manage something.

Mary smiled at him and handed him a cup of coffee.

"I thought you'd need lots of coffee, darling, after such a long drive."

"Yes, dear, I do. Thank you."

Just as he began to sip from his cup he glanced across the table at Mary. Her face had a peculiar expression. John was puzzled by it. They had been so close for so many years that she must be reading his mind. She must know what he was planning. Then she smiled; it was the glorious smile she had bestowed on him ever since their honeymoon. Everything was all right.

"Darling, excuse me for a minute," she said. "I just remembered something in the shop that I must see to. I'll be right back."

She walked quickly out of the dining room and across the hall into the shop.

But she didn't come back right away as she'd promised. If she didn't return soon John's coffee would be cold. He took a sip or two, then decided to go to the shop to see what had delayed Mary.

She didn't hear him enter. He found her in the middle room where the chandeliers were blazing. Her back was turned toward him and she was sitting on an Empire sofa close to the statues on their stands. She was ambushed by the statues.

Good lord, it was as he had suspected. She had been reading his thoughts. Her shoulders heaved. She was sobbing. She knew that their life together was ending. Then he decided that she might be laughing. Her shoulders would be shaking like that if she were laughing to herself. Whatever she was doing, whether she sobbed or laughed, it was no time for him to speculate on her mood. This was too good a chance to miss. With her head bent over she would be directly in the path of the bust of Victor Hugo or Benjamin Franklin or whoever it was towering above her. John would have to topple it only slightly and it would hit her skull. It needed only the gentlest shove.

He shoved.

It was so simple.

Poor darling girl. Poor Mary.

But it was all for the best and he wouldn't ever blame himself for what he'd done. Still, he was startled that it had been so easy, and it had taken no time at all. He would have tried it weeks before if he had known that it could be done with so little trouble.

John was quite composed. He took one last affectionate glance at Mary and then went back to the dining room. He would drink his coffee and then telephone the doctor. No doubt the doctor would offer to notify the police since it was an accidental death. John wouldn't need to lie about anything except for one slight detail. He would have to say that some movement of Mary's must have caused the bust to fall.

His coffee was still warm. He drank it unhurriedly. He thought of Lettice. He ached for the luxury of telephoning her that their life together was now assured and that after a discreet interval they could be married. But he decided he had better not take any chances. He would delay calling Lettice.

He felt joyful yet calm. He couldn't remember having felt so relaxed. No doubt it came from the relief of having done what had to be done. He was even sleepy. He was sleepier than he had ever been. He must lie down on the living-room couch. That was more urgent even than telephoning the doctor. But he couldn't wait to get to the couch. He laid his head on the dining table. His arms dangled.

None of Mary's and John's friends had any doubt about how the double tragedy had occurred. When they came to think of it, the shop had always been a booby trap, and that night Mary had tripped or stumbled and had toppled the statue onto her head. Then John had found her and grief had overwhelmed him. He realized he couldn't live without Mary, and his desperate sense of loss had driven him to dissolve enough sleeping tablets in his coffee to kill himself.

They all remembered so well how, in the middle of their last anniversary celebration, Mary and John had said they hoped they could die together. They really were the most devoted couple any of them had ever known. You could get sentimental just thinking about Mary and John, and to see them together was an inspiration. In a world of insecurity nothing was so heartening as their deep, steadfast love. It was sweet and touching that they had died on the same night, and exactly as they both had wanted.

YOU CAN'T BE TOO CAREFUL

by James Holding

Fargo Stott didn't find out until his murder trial was half over what was really at the bottom of the trouble he ran into when he tried to rob the Bronsons' house.

He had always been a pretty careful operator, as burglars go. Besides casing his jobs beforehand, he took the usual precautions any smart cat-man takes to reduce the natural hazards of his profession to manageable proportions: making sure a house was empty before breaking and entering; carrying a weapon for intimidation purposes; wearing a simple disguise to confuse any possible eyewitnesses.

And his batting average was a thousand percent until he tackled the Bronson job.

He cased that one with his usual thoroughness. And by the time he went into action he knew quite a bit about the Bronsons and their household. For one thing, he knew they qualified with an A-1 rating for his attention. They were rich and elderly; they both liked showy jewelry and wore a lot of it; they owned a collection of ancient Greek coins that would be worth a tidy sum even in the depressed market that Fargo would have to sell it in.

Furthermore, being fond of privacy presumably, the Bronsons lived alone except for a single houseman who had every Thursday off, disappearing regularly at noon Thursdays and never returning to the Bronsons' house until midnight or later. And, finally, the old-fashioned Bronson house was set well back from the street in a large lot that gave it isolation.

Well, Fargo saw Mr. and Mrs. Bronson leave their house one evening, all dressed up in evening clothes. *La Traviata* was opening in town that night, and Fargo knew that Mrs. Bronson was president of the local opera society. So he figured, rightly, that they were going to the opera. It was Thursday, their houseman's day off. And to Fargo, it looked like just the proper evening for him to dip into the Bronson cash, jewels and coin collection undisturbed.

He went back to his room and put on his disguise—several small pads that distorted his cheeks and eyes, a false beard, and elevator shoes that added two inches to his height. Then he strapped on his shoulder holster under his coat, made sure his automatic was loaded and resting easy in the leather, and started for the Bronsons' house.

On the way, he stopped off at a public telephone booth on the apron of a gas station and dialed the Bronsons' telephone number, with which he had prepared himself long before. He was pretty sure this was only a formality, since he'd seen the Bronsons leave their house, it was Thursday and, therefore, no one remained in the place to answer the phone. But Fargo was a careful man; he waited until the telephone had rung ten times without response before he hung up and left the booth.

He walked the remaining two blocks to the Bronson residence and, with a quick look around him, nipped into the yard and strode casually up the flagstone path through the garden to the front door. It was dark by this time; several lights were showing in the house. One burned over the entrance.

Boldly, Fargo stepped up to the front door and pressed the doorbell. Inside, musical chimes rang out. He waited, prepared, if anyone came, to ask where the Smiths lived, or was this the 700 block, or some other innocent question. He rang the chimes again, standing under the light in his elevator shoes. They pinched his feet a little.

No one came. Nothing happened. Nobody home.

Satisfied, Fargo found his way to the rear of the house. There were no neighbors close enough to overlook him. Contemptuous of noise, almost, he snapped a catch on a pantry window, lifted the sash and crawled into the house.

He stepped through a cluttered living room to the hallway and climbed the stairs to the second floor. It was arranged as many old houses are: a long narrow hall led from front to rear; along it, at intervals, were the doors leading to the upstairs rooms. Some of them were open, some closed. He ignored them. Mr. Bronson's den was at the end of the hall at the back—a large room lined with books on three walls. On the east side, stood the glass cases that housed the famous coin collection.

Switching on the den lights, Fargo went to the coin collection like a homing pigeon. He leaned over the nearest coin case and examined its rudimentary lock. Grinning, he picked that lock in less than two minutes and then, without haste, began to transfer the contents of the case to his pockets.

It was pleasant in Mr. Bronson's den. As he worked, Fargo noted with approval the red leather chair near the fireplace, the shaded reading lamps, and the framed photograph of a man (who was obviously Mr. Bronson's brother from the marked resemblance) that rested on a small table. The only sound audible in the house was the companionable clink of ancient Greek coins as he handled them.

Then suddenly, without warning, there was another sound. From where he stood in the den, Fargo couldn't see its source, but he was instantly certain what it was: the opening of one of the doors in that long hall behind him. It made a startling clamor in the silence.

He spun around toward the door of the den, mild concern working in him, nothing more. The door had been blown open by the wind, he told himself. Or nudged by a cat. It couldn't be anything else, or any*body* else. Impossible.

He still clutched some golden Greek coins in his right hand when a man appeared in the doorway of the den. In pajamas. A disreputable gray dressing gown. Tousled gray hair, sticking up in spikes. And the spitting image of—yes— the photograph there on the table. Mr. Bronson's brother!

For a moment, Fargo couldn't quite believe his eyes. Questions and answers flashed through his mind. Where did *he* spring from? A bedroom. What's he doing here? Visiting his brother. Why didn't I know of it? You can't watch a house twenty-four hours a day, you dope. And so on.

His eyes were on the bookshelves straight before him when he came into the room. Obviously, he wanted a book to read in bed. Then he saw Fargo. His eyes switched from Fargo's bearded face to the hand clutching the gold coins. Fargo could see comprehension dawn in his eyes.

Fargo, however, felt no real trepidation. After all, this guy had no weapon. He was far more surprised to see Fargo than Fargo was to see him. Now, Fargo told himself calmly, now while he's off balance is the time to get the jump. Show him the gun; lock him up in a closet; cut the telephone wires. And after that, there'll still be time to clean out the coin cases. The Bronsons won't be home for hours. And he can't tell what I look like through this beard.

Fargo stuffed the gold coins into a trouser pocket. Then he reached like a striking snake for his shoulder holster. But Bronson's brother didn't see him do it. For no sooner did it dawn on him that Fargo was a prowler than he turned in a swirl of shabby dressing gown and lunged down the hall away from the den. He was already in full career by the time Fargo got his gun out and leaped into the den doorway.

Fargo still felt only minor qualms about his position. He couldn't see any cause for deep concern. He had only to threaten the guy with his gun, he knew, and everything would be under control.

Bronson's brother was three yards away from Fargo, moving down the narrow hall toward the front of the house under a surprising head of steam, for such an old-timer, when Fargo yelled at him:

"Hold it, Dad! Come back here or I'll shoot you full of holes!"

Fargo expected that would stop him right away. It did no such thing. He put on more speed, if anything. Fargo was stunned.

Now, at last, he began to feel a faint stirring of panic; now, in less than a heartbeat's time, he began to doubt his control of the situation. He yelled again, louder than before, and sharper:

"Stop, damn you! You want a bullet in the back?"

Moved by an obscure impulse to catch and overpower the old man, Fargo ran down the long hallway after him, his automatic held out in front of him.

Bronson's brother didn't stop or even pause. Fargo began to wonder in a confused way just where the man thought he was running and what he was going to do when he got there. And all the time, Fargo kept yelling at him to stop or eat lead.

It wasn't long until Fargo knew where Bronson was going and why. He could see over the man's shoulder, at the front end of the hallway, the upstairs sitting room of the Bronsons' house with a wide window facing the street. This window was slightly open. And Bronson's brother at this moment began to do some yelling of his own.

"Help!" he bellowed. "Help! Police!" And he made so much racket that Fargo began to think that someone might actually hear him in spite of the isolation of the house. And what was worse, from Fargo's point of view, was that the man's own shouting was obviously preventing him from hearing Fargo's threats to shoot him in the back.

He was almost to the sitting room door when Fargo decided there was only one thing to do, only one way of bringing the old goat to his senses and making him realize the danger he was in.

Fargo held out his gun and squeezed off a shot, aiming, as well as he was able in his haste, toward the right side of the hallway and considerably behind the old man. That, Fargo thought angrily, should make the old fool realize I'm serious, that I've got a gun and will use it on him if I have to.

Then things happened very fast. Fargo was still, so he thought, chasing Bronson's brother down the hallway at top speed when suddenly he found himself tripping over him. Fargo fell headlong through the sitting-room doorway.

When he picked himself up and looked around, dazed and shaken, his automatic lost somewhere under a Victorian loveseat in the sitting room, he saw Mr. Bronson's brother lying on the floor of the hallway. His head was turned to one side. His arms were thrown out above his head. He was opening and closing his mouth as though he was still calling for help, but now he wasn't making a sound. Finally, Fargo saw the spreading red stain on the back of the shabby dressing gown between the old man's shoulders.

That's when the bitter realization came to Fargo, like a solid punch under the heart, that he'd shot the old boy in the back, just as he threatened he would—only with a bullet not meant to come anywhere near him. Nothing but terribly bad luck made the bullet ricochet from the wall of the hallway directly into his back.

Well, somebody *had* heard the yelling and the shot, it seemed. For Fargo was still fumbling ineffectually with the idea that he ought to get away from there in a hurry, when two policemen and the wide-eyed passerby who had raised the alarm, burst in on him.

They found Mr. Bronson's brother dead at Fargo's feet.

And Fargo didn't find out until Mr. Bronson gave his testimony at the trial what it was that really caused the Bronson job to go so sour.

Mr. Bronson's brother had been stone deaf.

MURDER DELAYED

by Henry Slesar

"Certainly is a warm day," the reporter said. "Mind if I open this window some more?"

"Go ahead," Joe Harper said. He got up slowly from the chair and went cautiously to the liquor cabinet. When he poured the drink, a tall, cool one, his actions were stiff and deliberate. The reporter, knowing the reason, watched him with pained eyes.

"You don't have to bother," he said.

"No trouble," Harper answered. "I can still get around okay, long as I take it easy." He brought him the drink, and smiled. The smile didn't relax the taut, thin face. It faded as soon as Harper lowered his gaunt body into the chair again. He was a man in his late forties, and except for the evidence of suffering, his small features and dark hair might have made him look younger.

"I suppose you've told the story often," the reporter said. "I certainly appreciate you giving me the time."

"Not so often. At first, when the robbery happened, and during the trial, a lot of newspapers were interested. Then, as soon as Nally was convicted and sent up, everybody seemed to forget. You say this'll be a Sunday feature?"

"That's right. The human side, you know?"

"Yes," Harper said.

"I never thought anything like this would happen when I went to work for Mr. Pachman," Harper said. "He was such a mild old guy, with such a small business. In the same building where Pachman had his little diamond-buying and -selling company, there must have been fifty big-time dealers. But maybe that's what made the job attractive to Nally. Maybe he thought the old man's place would be a pushover.

"After I was there a couple of months, I was handling most of the customer transactions even though Pachman did all the appraisal work himself. He must have been seventy, and he wasn't up to much effort. Most weeks, he would only come to the office two or three days. He wasn't in the day Nally decided to make his move.

"It was a Tuesday morning, and I had just sent Ruthie, the office secretary, out to get me some coffee. That left me alone in the place when this young guy in the jazzy sports jacket came in. I wasn't put off by the outfit; you should see some of the ratty-looking customers we got, some of them with thousands of dollars' worth of diamonds in their pockets. But I got suspicious when he started to stammer at me about making a purchase. He finally made it clear that he wanted to look at some emerald-cut stones for an engagement ring. I took out a tray, but I put it down on the counter near the foot alarm. He must have known what I was up to right away, because that's when he brought out the gun.

"To tell you the truth, I was too scared to give him any kind of argument. It wasn't my business, after all, and I knew Pachman was insured, and what was the use of getting myself killed? I watched him scoop up the diamonds on the tray, and then he asked me to get some more from the drawers. He was shaking pretty bad, and so was I. When I brought out the second tray, my fingers couldn't hold on to it, and I dropped it on the floor. When I bent down to pick up the scattered stones, my hand got pretty close to the alarm button and he must have thought I was double-crossing him. That's when he shot me.

"I didn't remember much after that, except that I heard the door slamming when he ran out. Then I was unconscious and woke up for a few seconds in the ambulance. I also have a vague recollection of going down the hospital corridor, flat on my back, watching the ceiling lights go by as they wheeled me into the operating room. It was only when I came out of sedation three hours later that I was able to talk to the police, and learned that Nally had been nabbed on the way out of the building. There was only one exit, you know, all those diamond buildings on 47th Street have only one way in and out. But it was the next day before I learned that they had been unable to remove the bullet Nally put in me.

"That was the rough part. The slug had hit me in the chest and just missed the heart and lung. But it was lodged in such a place that there was no way to remove it without the danger of puncturing one vital organ or another. They showed me the X rays, and gave me nice long lectures about anatomy, and I began to understand that the odds were pretty good that the bullet would be jolted loose some day and kill me.

"I was still in the hospital when Nally was arraigned for the robbery and shooting. I was seeing a lot of people then. Specialists who came around to cluck over the X rays and shake their heads. Reporters who wanted to know how I felt about carrying around a death sentence in my chest. Then, finally, they brought Nally himself for me to identify. I recognized him, all right.

"By the time his trial came up, the hospital decided they couldn't do me any more good, so I was released. I was told to be cautious, to take it easy, to refrain from all strenuous activity. The quieter I was, the more chance I had to go on living. But it was only phony reassurance, I knew that. That bullet was going to get me. In a week, in a month, maybe even a year, but I was a dead man.

"The district attorney asked if I'd testify at the trial. I said sure. I wanted to see Nally get the works, and I was the guy who could make sure he did. I'll never forget that day. Nally had half the courtroom filled with his relatives, and they were all weeping and carrying on like the trial was a wake. Seems he came from one of those big, loyal, close-knit families. The judge had to clear the courtroom, they made so much noise. The defense attorney tried to make a case for Nally's youth. But once I got up on the stand, he was cooked.

"Well, you know the way the verdict read. Nally got thirty years. He was a murderer, and he deserved the chair, but technically the law couldn't give him his full punishment, not while I was still walking around and breathing.

"But that was only temporary. He wasn't going to get off so light. If it wasn't for that bullet in me, he could have served out his sentence, maybe even gotten a parole before he was an old man. But there was this bullet. And one of these days, it was going to kill me. And when it did, Nally was going to be a killer, facing a murder charge.

"It's funny, huh? That guy's sitting up in Ossining right now, praying for my health. But according to the docs, his prayers won't do any good and neither will mine. Once I go, he gets arraigned all over again, this time for murder in the first degree. It won't be double jeopardy, either; the D.A. squelched that. It'll be an entirely different charge, and Nally won't be able to get away with it.

"So that's my only consolation. When my time comes, so does Nally's. When I die, he dies. It's not much to be happy about—but when you're in my kind of fix, you've got to be satisfied with anything."

Joe Harper had been pacing the room as he talked, moving slowly, carefully. He stopped at the open window and looked out. Dusk was descending, and a few stars were making their appearance in the purple sky. He glanced up at them, and sighed.

"It's tough," the reporter said gravely. "I'm really sorry, Mr. Harper. But if anything, it's probably even tougher on Frank Nally."

"You think I care about him?" Harper sneered.

"No," the reporter said. "I guess you don't." He came up behind Harper and took his elbow. "I'm sorry," he said again. He pushed Harper off balance, and Harper looked at him in surprise. It was only two steps to the window, and when Harper felt himself teetering on the edge of nothing he gaped at the intense young face in hope of either mercy or explanation.

"I'm not a reporter," the man said. "I'm Nally's brother." And Joe Harper, doomed to one death or another, went to his end on the sidewalk below.

PATTERN OF GUILT

by Helen Nielsen

Keith Briscoe had never been a hating man. Disciplined temper, alert mind, hard work—these were the things that made for success as a police reporter, and in the fourteen years since he'd returned from overseas, too big for his old suits and his old job as copy boy, Keith Briscoe had become one of the best. Enthusiasm was a help—something close to passion at times, for that was the stuff brilliance was made of—but not hatred. Hatred was a cancer in the mind, a dimness in the eye. Hatred was an acid eating away the soul. Keith Briscoe was aware of all these things, but he was becoming aware of something else as well. No matter how hard he forced the thought to the back of his mind, he knew that he hated his wife. And the thought was sharp, clear.

It was Sergeant Gonzales' case—burglary and murder. Violet Hammerman, thirty-eight, lived alone in a single apartment on North Curson. She worked as a secretary in a small manufacturing plant from Monday through Friday, played bridge with friends on Saturday night, served on the Hostess Committee of her church Sunday morning and died in her bed Sunday night (Monday morning, to be exact, since it was after 2 A.M. when the crime occurred), the victim of one bullet through her heart fired at close range. Sergeant Gonzales was a thorough man, and by the time Keith Briscoe reached the scene, having responded with fire-horse reflexes to the homicide code on his shortwave receiver, all of these matters, and certain others, were already established and Gonzales was waiting for the police photographer to complete his chores so the body could be removed to the morgue.

She wasn't a pretty woman. A corpse is seldom attractive.

"You can see for yourself," Gonzales said. "It's a simple story. No struggle, no attempted attack—the bedclothes aren't even disturbed. The neighbors heard her scream once and then the shot came immediately afterward. She should have stayed asleep."

She was asleep now. Nothing would ever rouse her again. Briscoe glanced at the bureau drawer that was still standing half-open. One nylon stocking dangled forlornly over the side. He fingered it absently and then, without touching the wood, stuffed it inside.

"Fingerprints?" he asked.

"No fingerprints," Gonzales said. "The killer must have worn gloves, but he left a pair of footprints outside the window."

There was only one window in the small bedroom. It was a first-floor apartment in one of the old residential houses that had been rezoned and remodeled into small units, but still had a shallow basement and a correspondingly high footing. Violet Hammerman must have felt secure to sleep with her one window open and the screen locked, but that had been a mistake. The screen had been neatly cut across the bottom and up as far as the center sash on both sides. It now hung like a stiffly starched curtain, that bent outward at the touch of Keith Briscoe's hand.

"Port of entry and exit."

"That's right," Gonzales said. "But the exit was fast. He must have made a running jump out of the window and landed on the cement drive. It was the entry that left the prints. Collins, shoot your flash under the window again."

Collins was the man in uniform who stood guarding the important discovery beneath the window. He responded to Gonzales order by pointing a bright finger of light down on the narrow strip of earth that separated the house from the driveway. It was a plot barely eighteen inches wide, but somebody had worked it over for planting, and because of that a pair of footprints was distinctly visible on the soft earth.

"We're in luck," Gonzales explained. "The landlord worked that ground yesterday morning. Set out some petunia plants —ruffled petunias. Too bad. A couple of them will never bloom."

A couple of them were slightly demolished from trampling, but between the withered green the two indentations were embedded, like an anonymous signature. Briscoe shoved the screen forward and peered farther out of the window.

"It must be nearly six feet to the ground," he remarked.

"Sixty-eight inches," Gonzales said.

"The footprints don't seem very deep."

"They aren't—no heels. If you were down where Collins is, you'd see what I saw a few minutes before you walked in. Those prints are from rubber-soled shoes, 'sneakers' we used to call them when I was a kid. At closer view you can pick up the imprint of some of the tread, but not much. Those particular soles were pretty well worn. But you're thinking, Briscoe, as usual. That earth is soft. We'll have to measure the moisture content to get an idea of how much weight stood above those prints to make them the depth they are, but at first guess I'd say we're looking for a tall, slender lad."

"A juvenile?" Briscoe asked.

"Why not? Like I told my wife when she came home from her shopping trip last week, no wonder so many kids are going wrong. They come home from school and find their mothers dressed up in a sack with a belt at the bottom. That's enough to drive anyone out on the streets."

Keith Briscoe pulled his head in out of the window and ran a searching hand over the cut screen. It was a clean job. A sharp blade of a pocket knife could do the job. Gonzales could be right about the juvenile angle.

"You sound like a detective," he said.

"Gee, thanks," Gonzales grinned. "Maybe I'll grow up to be a hot reporter some day. Who can tell?"

There was no sarcasm in the exchange. Gonzales and Briscoe had been friends long enough to be able to insult one another with respect and affection. Gonzales had a good mind and an eye for detail. He also had imagination, which was to building a police case what mortar is to a bricklayer.

"We found a purse—black felt—on the driveway near the curb," he added. "People in the building identified it as belonging to the deceased. There's no money in it except some small change in the coin purse, but there's this that we found on the top of the bureau—"

Gonzales had a slip of blue paper in his hand. He handed it to Briscoe. It was the deduction slip from a company paycheck. After deductions, Violet Hammerman had received a check for $61.56.

"Payday was Friday," Gonzales continued. "The landlord told me that. He knows because he's had to wait for his rent a few times. Violet Hammerman didn't have time to get to the bank Friday—she worked late—but she cashed her check at the Sav-Mor Market on Saturday." Gonzales had another slip of paper in his hand now, a long, narrow strip from a cash register. "When she bought groceries to the sum of $14.82," he added.

There was such a thing as sounding too much like a detective. Briscoe returned the blue slip with a dubious expression. It was barely two-thirty. Gonzales was a fast worker, but the markets didn't open until nine. But Gonzales caught the expression before he could fit it with words.

"I'm guessing, of course," he said quickly, "but I'm guessing for a reason. $14.82 from $61.56 leaves $46.74. Assuming she spent a few dollars elsewhere and dropped a bill in the collection plate, we see that Violet Hammerman's killer escaped with the grand sum of $40 or, at the most, $45."

"A cheap death," Briscoe said.

"A very cheap death, and a very cheap and amateurish killer." Gonzales paused to glance at the slip of blue paper again, but it was no longer entirely blue. A red smear had been added to the corner. "What did you do, cut your hand on that screen?" he asked.

Briscoe didn't know what he was talking about, but he looked at his hand and it was bleeding.

"Better look in the bathroom for some mercurochrome," Gonzales said. "You could get a nasty infection from a rusty screen."

"It's nothing," Briscoe said. "I'll wash it off under the faucet when I get home."

"You'll wash it off under the faucet right now," Gonzales ordered. "There's the bathroom on the other side of the bureau."

Gonzales could be as fussy as a spinster. It was easier to humor him than to argue. The photographer was finished with the corpse now, and Briscoe pulled the sheet up over her face as he walked past the bed. A cheap death and a cheap way to wait for the ambulance. Violet Hammerman had lived a humble and inconspicuous life, but she might rate a conspicuous obituary if he could keep Gonzales talking. Of course, Violet Hammerman might not have approved of such an obituary, but she now belonged to the public.

"A cheap and amateurish killer," Briscoe said, with his hand under the faucet, "but he wore gloves, rubber-soled shoes and carried a gun."

Leaning against the bathroom doorway, Gonzales rose to the bait.

"Which he fired too soon," he said. "That's my point, Briscoe. There's a pattern in every crime—something that gives us an edge on the criminal's weakness, and we know he has a weakness or he wouldn't be a criminal. It takes a mind, some kind of a mind, to plan a burglary; but it takes nerve to pull it off successfully. This killer is very short on nerve. One cry from the bed and he blazed away at close range. A professional wouldn't risk the gas chamber for a lousy forty bucks. Don't use that little red towel. Red dye's no good for an open cut."

Gonzales, with an eye for detail even when his mind was elsewhere. Briscoe put the guest towel back on the rack. A silly-looking thing—red with a French poodle embroidered in black. It seemed out of place in Violet Hammerman's modest bathroom. It was more the sort of thing Elaine would buy. Elaine. He thought of her and slammed the faucet shut so hard the plumbing pipes shuddered.

"A killer short on nerve, but desperate enough to break into a house." Briscoe recapitulated, his mind busy forcing Elaine back where she belonged. "A forty-dollar murder." And then he had what he was groping for, and by that time he could face Gonzales without fear of anger showing in his face. "Sounds like a hophead," he suggested.

Gonzales nodded sadly.

"That's what I've been thinking," he said. "That's what worries me. How much of a joyride can he buy for so little fare? I only hope Violet Hammerman isn't starting a trend."

Among his other characteristics, Sergeant Gonzales was a pessimist, and Keith Briscoe couldn't give him any cheer. He had troubles of his own.

Judge Kermit Lacy's court hadn't changed in four years. The flag stood in the same place; the woodwork still needed varnishing; the chairs were just as hard. If the windows had been washed, the evidence was no longer visible. Courtrooms could be exciting arenas where combatting attorneys fought out issues of life and death, but there was nothing exciting about a courtroom where tired old loves went to die, or to be exhumed for delayed postmortem.

The dead should stay dead. The thought tugged at Keith Briscoe's mind when he saw Faye sitting at her attorney's table. Faye had changed in four years. She looked younger, yet more mature, more poised. She wore a soft gray suit and a hat that was smart without being ridiculous. There had never been anything ridiculous about Faye—that was the only trouble with her; she always carried with her the faint aura of Old Boston. She looked up and saw him then. And when their eyes met, there was a kind of stop on time for just an instant, an almost imperceptible shadow crossed her eyes, and then she smiled. Keith walked to the table. He didn't quite know what to do. Was it customary to shake hands with an ex-wife—the sort of thing tennis players do after vaulting the net? He kept his hands at his side.

"You're looking good, Faye," he said, "—great, in fact." Clumsy words, as if he were just learning the language.

"Thank you," Faye responded. "You look well, too, Keith. You've lost weight."

Keith started to say "No more home cooking" and thought better of it. And he didn't look well. It wasn't just because he'd been up most of the night delving into the violent departure of one Violet Hammerman from this vale of fears; it was because he had that depth-fatigue look of a man who's gradually working up to an extended hangover.

"I keep busy," he said.

"And how is Elaine?"

That question had to come. Keith searched in vain for a twinge of emotion in Faye's voice. There was none. Elaine was a knife that had cut between them a long time ago, and old wounds heal.

"Elaine's fine," he said, and then he couldn't be evasive any longer. "Faye—" The bailiff had entered the courtroom. In a few moments the judge would walk in and there would be no more time to talk. "—I wish you'd reconsider this action. We have a good arrangement now. If you take the boys east, I'll never get to see them."

"But that's not true," Faye objected. "They can visit with you on vacations."

"Vacations! A few weeks out of a year—that's not like every weekend!"

"Every weekend, Keith?" Faye's voice was soft, but her eyes were steady. Faye's eyes were always steady. "You've had four years of weekends to visit the boys. How many times have you taken advantage of them?"

"Every weekend I possibly could! You know how my job is!"

Faye knew. The half-smile that came to her lips had a sadness in it. Now that he really looked at her, Keith could see the sadness. She was lonely. She must be lonely, bringing up two boys with nothing but an alimony check for companionship. Now she was bringing suit for permission to take the boys east—ostensibly to enroll them in prep school; but Keith Briscoe suddenly knew the real reason. There were old friends back east to wipe out the memories—perhaps even an old flame.

Keith felt a quick jab of pain he didn't understand.

"I'm going to fight you, Faye," he said. "I'm sorry, but I'm going to fight you every inch of the way."

It was nearly eight o'clock that night before Keith got home to his apartment. Nobody came to greet him at the door except Gus, Elaine's dachshund. Gus growled at him, which was standard procedure, and made a couple of wild snaps at his ankles as he passed through the dark living room and made his way to the patch of brightness showing down the hall. At the doorway of Elaine's bedroom, he paused and listened to the music coming from the record player at her bedside. It was something Latin with a very low spinal beat. He listened to it until she came out of the bathroom wearing something French with an equally low spinal beat. Keith was no couturier, but he could see at a glance that Elaine's dress wasn't percale and hadn't been designed for a quiet evening at home. He could also see that it was expensive. He would know how expensive at the first of the month.

She looked up and saw him in the doorway.

"Oh," she said. "I didn't hear you come in."

Keith didn't answer immediately. He just stood there looking at her—all of her, outside and inside. The outside was still attractive. He could feel the tug of her body clear across the room.

"Do you ever?" he asked.

Elaine turned around and picked up an ear clip from her dressing table. She raised her arms to fasten it to her ear.

"Going out?" he asked again.

"It's Thelma's birthday," she said.

"I thought it was Thelma's birthday last week."

That made her turn around.

"All right," she said, "what's eating you? Have you been playing with martinis again?"

"I'm old enough," Keith said. He came across the room. She not only looked good, she smelled good. "I just thought you might want to stay home for one evening."

"Why? So I can sit in the dark alone and watch Wyatt Earp? This lousy apartment—"

"This lousy apartment," Keith interrupted, "costs me $175 every month. Considering certain other expenditures I have to meet, it's no wonder I devote a little extra time to doing what is known among the peasants as being gainfully employed. If I didn't, you couldn't look so provocative for Thelma's birthday."

Elaine picked up the other ear clip and fastened it in place. It was as though he hadn't spoken, hadn't reprimanded her. And then her face in the mirror took on a kind of animal cunning. She turned back toward him with knowing eyes.

"How did you make out in court?" she asked.

"We got a continuance," Keith said.

"A continuance? Why? So you can suffer a little longer?"

"I want my boys—"

"You want Faye! Why can't you be honest enough to admit it? You've always wanted Faye. You only married me because you couldn't have your cake and eat it, too. That's your big weakness, Keith. You want to have your cake and eat it, too!"

"I want a divorce," Keith said.

He hadn't meant to say it—not yet, not this way. But once it was said, there was nothing to do but let the words stand there like a wall between them, or like a wall with a door in it that was opening. And then Elaine slammed the door.

"You," she said quietly, "can go to hell."

That was the night Keith Briscoe moved out of the apartment. He'd been spending most of his nights in a furnished room anyway, a room, a bath, a hot plate for the coffee and a desk for his typewriter. And a table for the short-wave radio alongside the bed. The typewriter had bothered Elaine at night, and that was when Keith did most of his work. He could pick up extra money turning police cases into fabrications for the mystery magazines. Extra money was important with two boys growing their way toward college.

But on the night he moved into the room to stay, Keith didn't work. He just sat and stared at the calendar on the desk and tried to get things straight in his mind. He had a one week's continuance. One week until he'd walk back into Judge Lacy's courtroom and see Faye sitting there calm and proud and lonely. Elaine was a stupid woman, but even the biggest fools made sense when the time was right. It was Faye that he wanted—Faye, the boys, everything that he'd thrown away. Elaine was a bad dream. Elaine was an emotional storm he'd been lost in, and now the storm was over and he was trying to find his way home through the debris. But a week wasn't very long. Perhaps his lawyer could find a loophole and get another stay. It was actually only six days until Monday. . . .

On Sunday night, at a half hour past midnight, the short-wave radio rousted him out again.

Dorothy McGannon had a cheerful face even in death. She must have smiled a lot in life. Once her moment of terror was over, the muscles of her face had relaxed into their normal position, and she might have been sleeping through a happy dream if it hadn't been for the dark stain seeping through the blanket.

She was alone in the room, except for Sergeant Gonzales and company. She had lived alone, an unmarried woman in her late twenties. The apartment was small—living room, kitchen, and bedroom. It was on the second floor, rear, one of eight apartments in the unit. The service landing stopped about eighteen inches from the window where the screen was cut three ways and now poked awkwardly out into the night. It had taken agility to balance on the railing and slit that screen; it had taken even more to swing out onto the railing and escape after the fatal shot had been fired.

"Our boy's getting daring," Gonzales reflected. "Still nervous with the trigger, but daring."

"Do you think it's the same killer who got Violet Hammerman last week?" Keith asked.

Up until this point, nobody had mentioned Violet Hammerman. She was just last week's headline, forgotten by everyone but next of kin. But the cut screen and swift death were familiar. Gonzales, the pattern-maker, was already at work.

"That was a .45 slug ballistics got out of the Hammerman

woman," he answered. "When we see what killed this one, I'll give you a definite answer. Unfortunately, there's no soft earth out on that porch landing—no footprints; but the method of entry is the same. That's a peculiar way to cut a screen, you know. It takes longer that way."

"But makes for a safer exit," Keith said.

"That's true—and this caller always leaves in a hurry." Gonzales turned back toward the bed, scowling. "I wonder if he kills them just for the fun of it," he mused. "Nobody heard a scream tonight. The shot, but no scream. Still, with five out of eight television sets still going, it's a wonder they heard anything."

"Did he get what he came for?" Keith asked.

Still scowling, Gonzales turned and looked at him. Then he nodded his head in a beckoning gesture.

"Follow me," he said.

They crossed the small bedroom and went into the living room. They turned to the right and entered the kitchen alcove, which had one wall common to the bedroom and faced the living room door. The far wall of the kitchen was cupboard space, and one door stood open. On the sink top, laying on its side as if it had been opened hurriedly, was a sugar can which contained no sugar—or anything else.

"What does that look like?" Gonzales asked.

"It looks like Dorothy McGannon kept her money in a sugar can," Keith said.

"Exactly. She worked as a legal secretary. She was paid Friday and gave $10 to the manager of this place Friday night in payment for $10 she'd borrowed earlier in the week. He saw a roll of bills in her purse at the time—$50 or $60, he thinks. We found the purse in a bureau drawer in the bedroom—there was $5 and some change in it."

"The killer missed it."

"The killer didn't even look for it. That drawer stuck—it made enough noise to wake the dead, well, almost. It's obvious he didn't bother with the bureau, and that's interesting because it's what he did bother with last week. Instead, he came straight to the kitchen, opened the cupboard door, and now it's bare."

What Sergeant Gonzales was saying explained the frown that had grown on his forehead. It meant another piece of the pattern of guilt was being fitted to an unknown killer.

"He might have been a friend of the woman," Keith said,

"—someone who had been in the apartment and knew where she kept the money. A boyfriend, possibly. She was single."

"So was the Hammerman woman," Gonzales reflected. "But no boyfriend. We questioned the landlord about that, definitely no boyfriend. But you're right, she was single. They were both single and both killed on Sunday night. It's beginning to add up, isn't it? Two murders, each victim a woman who lived alone, each one killed on a weekend after a Friday payday. Do you want to lay a small bet that's a .45 slug in the corpse?"

"No bet," Keith said. "What about groceries?"

"Groceries? What groceries?"

"McGannon's. Does she have any? Hammerman did, as I recall. Over $14.00 worth."

Gonzales looked interested. He glanced behind him at the living-room door clearly visible from the kitchen.

"You're thinking again, Briscoe," he said. "A delivery boy—but wait, Hammerman's groceries were paid for at the market. Still, it might have been a delivery boy. Tall, skinny. The lab says not over 150 pounds. It's worth looking into. I don't like the idea of a murder every weekend."

Dorothy McGannon did Keith a big favor getting herself killed when she did. It was a good enough story to keep him away from court until another continuance had been called, and that meant another week to try to reach Faye. He caught her coming down the courthouse steps. She was annoyed that he hadn't shown up—obviously, she thought it was deliberate, and Keith wasn't certain but what she was right.

"If we can go somewhere and have a drink, I'll explain," he suggested.

"I'm sorry, Keith. I've wasted enough time as it is."

"But I couldn't help not showing. I was on a big story—look."

He unfolded the late edition and handed it to her. She hesitated.

"One drink to show there's no hard feelings," Keith said.

She consented, finally. It wasn't a warm consent, but Keith took it as a major victory. He drove her to a small bar near the news building where she used to meet him in the old days, when their marriage, and the world, was young. Faye had always been a little on the sentimental side. He led the way to their old booth at the back of the room and ordered a Scotch on the rocks and a Pink Lady. That was supposed to indicate that he hadn't forgotten.

"Make it a vodka martini," Faye said.

"You've changed drinks," Keith observed.

"I've changed a lot of things, Keith."

That was true. Now that they were alone, he could see it. This wasn't going to be easy. Faye took a cigarette from her purse. He fumbled in his pocket for a lighter, and then studied the situation in her eyes, lustrous over the flame.

"I've changed, too," he told her. "I'm working nights now, Faye. Real industrious. I've been doing a little writing on the side—may even get at that novel I used to talk about."

"That's good," Faye said. "I'm glad to hear it." And then she paused. "How does Elaine like it?"

Keith snapped the lighter shut and played it back and forth in his hands.

"Elaine and I aren't living together any more," he said. "I moved out last week."

He watched for a reaction, but Faye was good at concealing emotions. She was like the proverbial iceberg—nine-tenths submerged. If he'd realized that four years sooner, he wouldn't have been sitting there like a troubled schoolboy waiting for the report on a test paper.

"I'm sorry, Keith," she said.

"I'm not. It's been coming for a long time. It was a mistake from the beginning—the whole mess. I don't know how I could have been so blind."

One drink together. He didn't say much more; he didn't dare push her. Faye was the kind who would walk away from him the minute he did. But at least he had said the important things, and she could think about them for another week.

Not until he was back in that small, furnished room did it occur to Keith that he was playing the fool. He was trying to get Faye back when he didn't even know how to get rid of Elaine. He sat down to work. He pushed the problem back in his mind and concentrated on Sergeant Gonzales' problem. The case was beginning to fascinate him. What kind of a killer was it who would operate in this way? A half-crazy hophead, yes; but with enough animal cunning to make some kind of plan of operation. Now he understood what Gonzales meant by that pattern talk. If it were possible to think as the killer thought . . . Obviously, he'd been in Dorothy McGannon's apartment prior to the murder. Very few people kept household money in sugar cans any more. Elaine kept money anywhere—scattered about the bedroom in half a dozen purses. The "cat-killer," as Keith had dubbed him in his latest story, would have a holiday if he slashed her window screen.

But how would he know? He thought of Elaine again—she wouldn't stay in the back of his mind. He thought of her alone in the apartment. What did she do all day? She never went to the market; she telephoned for groceries. But she didn't pay for them, except to give the delivery boy a tip. The bill, along with many, many others, came in at the first of the month. There were other deliveries: the cleaner, the liquor store . . . And what else? And then he remembered that in the early days of their marriage, before Elaine learned to go outside for her amusements, she'd been a pushover for all the gadgets peddled by the door-to-door trade. It was a thought, and an impelling one.

A gadget. It would have to be something easy to sell; getting the door slammed in his face wouldn't help the killer at all. He had to have a few minutes, at least, to size up the possibilities: learn if the woman lived alone, see where she went for the money when he made the sale. Perhaps he had a gimmick—the "I just need 100 more points" routine. There were other approaches, legitimate ones that could have been borrowed: items made by the blind, items made by the crippled or mentally retarded. Something a woman would buy whether she needed it or not.

The next day, Keith went to Gonzales with his idea. Together they paid another visit to the McGannon woman's apartment. They examined the drawers in that kitchen cupboard—all standard items from bottle opener to egg beater, but nothing that looked new. Gonzales moved to the broom closet.

"Sometimes peddlers handle cosmetic items," Keith reflected. "I'll have a look in the bathroom."

He went through the tiny bedroom and into an even tinier bath. There was no tub, just a stall shower and a pullman lavatory. He pulled open one of the lavatory drawers and then called to Gonzales. When Gonzales came into the room,

Keith stood with a small guest towel in his hand. It was green this time, a sort of chartreuse green with a black French poodle embroidered at the bottom.

"Familiar?" he asked.

And Gonzales remembered, because a red towel was bad for an open cut.

They made an inquiry at every apartment in the building where anyone was at home. Afterwards, they went to the apartment on Curson and interviewed all of the available tenants there. Out of it all, a picture emerged. In both cases, on the Saturday prior to the murder, at least one tenant at each address remembered seeing a peddler with a basket on his arm entering the premises. One tenant at the Hammerman address, an elderly woman living with her retired husband, actually stopped the peddler on the walk and conversed with him.

"He was selling little towels and things," she reported. "Real pretty and cheap, too. I bought two for a quarter apiece. Would have bought more, but a pension don't go far these days." But did she remember how the peddler looked? Indeed, she did. A tall, gawky young man—hardly more than a boy. "Not much of a salesman," she added. "He didn't even seem to care about selling his things. I had to stop him or he would have gone right past my door."

He had gone right past all of the doors, apparently, except two—Violet Hammerman's and Dorothy McGannon's. A check on the mail boxes at each unit indicated an explanation. All of the other apartments in each building were occupied by two or more tenants. The cat killer concentrated on women living alone.

"That's great," Gonzales concluded. "In this particular area we have the largest concentration of unmarried people of any section of the city. Now all we have to do is locate every woman living alone and warn her not to buy a guest towel from a door-to-door peddler."

"Aren't peddlers licensed?" Keith said.

"Licensed peddlers are licensed," Gonzales said. "But what's more important, merchandise of this sort is manufactured. There's a code number on the tag inside. Keep your hat on this operation for a few days, Briscoe, and you may have an exclusive. In the meantime, this whole area will be searched for a tall, thin peddler carrying a basket."

"Or not carrying a basket," Keith suggested. "I don't think

your man entered these buildings blind. I think he had his
victims selected days before the Saturday checkup. I think
he watched them, studied the location of the apartments—
planned everything in advance. He's probably out lining up
next Sunday night's target right now. He's making headlines,
Gonzales. Everybody has an ego."

Gonzales made no argument.

"You've really been doing some head work on this," he
said.

"Yes," Keith answered, "I have."

There was more head work to do.

Keith went shopping. He left Gonzales and found his way
to one of the large department stores. He located the linen
department and wandered about the aisles, avoiding sales-
ladies until he found what he was looking for: guest towels
in all the assorted colors, guest towels with jaunty French
poodles embroidered at the bottom.

"Something for you, sir?"

A voice at his shoulder brought his mind back to the moment.

"No, no thanks," he said. "I was just looking."

He walked away quickly. He was doing too much head
work; he needed some air.

That evening he went to see Elaine. He still had his key
and could let himself in. Nobody met him at the door, not
even Gus.

"He's at the vet's," Elaine explained. "He caught a cold.
They're keeping him under observation for a week."

She was in the bedroom doing her nails. She sat on the
bed, sprawled back against the pillows. She barely looked at
him when she spoke.

"I thought you weren't coming back," she said.

"I'm not," he told her. "I only came tonight so we could
talk things over."

"Talk? What is there to talk about?"

"A divorce."

The hand operating the nail-polish brush hesitated a moment.

"We did talk about that—last week," Elaine said.

He waited for several seconds and there was no sign of
interest in his presence. He might have been a piece of furniture she was ready to give to the salvage truck. He walked

past the bed and over to the window. Elaine's carpet was thick; he couldn't have heard his footsteps with a stethoscope. He went to the window and pulled aside the soft drapes. It was a casement window and both panels were cranked out to let in the night air. The apartment was on the second floor. Directly below, the moonlight washed over the flat roof of the long carport and caught on the smooth curve of the service ladder spilling over the side. The window itself was a scant five feet above the roof.

"You should keep this window locked," he said. "It's dangerous this way."

The change of subject brought her eyes up from her nails. "What do you mean?"

"Haven't you been reading the papers?"

"Oh, that!"

"It's nothing to scoff at. Two women are very dead."

She stared at him then, because this wasn't just conversation and she was beginning to know it.

"Stop wishing so hard," she said. "You're almost drooling."

"Don't be stupid, Elaine."

"I'm not stupid—and I'm not going to let you scare me into letting you off the hook. What do you think I am, Keith? A substitute wife you can use for a while until you decide to go back to the home-fires and slippers routine? Well, I'm not! I told you before, you can't have your cake and eat it. You walked out on me—I didn't send you away. Just try to get a divorce on that and see what it costs you!"

It was two days later that Sergeant Gonzales called Keith to his office. There had been a new development in the case, one of those unexpected breaks that could mean everything or nothing, depending on how it went. A call had come in from a resident of a court in West Hollywood. A woman had reported seeing a prowler outside her bedroom windows. Bedroom windows were a critical area with Gonzales by this time, and when it developed that the woman lived alone, worked five days a week and spent weekends at home, what might have been a routine complaint became important enough for a personal interview. True to his words, he was cutting Keith in on the story if there was one, and there was.

Nettie Swanson was a robust, middle-aged woman of definite opinions on acceptable and inacceptable human conduct.

"I don't like snoopers," she reported. "If anybody's curious about how I live, let him come to the door and ask. Snoopers I can't abide. That's why I called the police when I saw this fellow hanging around out back."

"Can you describe the man, Miss Swanson," Gonzales asked.

"I sure can. He was tall—like a beanpole. Would have been taller if he hadn't slouched so much. Young, too. Not that I really saw his face, but I thought he must be young by the way he slouched. Can you give me any reason why young folks today walk around like they been hit in the stomach? And their faces! All calf-eyed like a bunch of strays trying to find their way back to the barn!"

"Miss Swanson," Gonzales cut in, "how are your nerves?"

Some people talked big and folded easily. Nettie Swanson was as collapsible as a cast iron accordian. She listened to Sergeant Gonzales explain the situation and a fire began to kindle in her eyes. The prowler might come back, he told her. He might appear at her door sometime Saturday carrying a basket of items to sell. Would she allow a police officer to wait in her apartment and nab him?

"That's not necessary," she said. "I got a rifle back in my closet that I used to shoot rattlesnakes with when I was a girl in Oklahoma. I can handle that prowler."

"But he's not just a prowler," Gonzales protested. "If he's the man we think he is, he's already killed two women that we know of."

She took the information soberly. She wasn't blind, and she could read. And then her eyes brightened again as the truth sank home.

"The 'cat-killer'! Now, isn't that something! Well, in that case I guess I'd better leave things to you, Sergeant. But I've got my rifle if you need another gun."

Gonzales couldn't have found a more cooperative citizen.

Saturday. Keith sat with Gonzales in a small, unmarked sedan across the street from the apartment house where Nettie Swanson lived. It was an old two-story affair flanked on one side by a new multiple unit and on the other by a shaggy hedge that separated the edge of the lot from a narrow alleyway. The hedge was at least five feet high and only the mouth of the alleyway was visible from the sedan. But the entrance to the building was visible and had been visible for over an hour. Inside the building, one of Gonzales' men had been waiting since nine o'clock. It was nearly eleven.

Keith was perspiring. He opened the door next to him to let a little more air into the sedan. Gonzales watched him with curious eyes.

"You're even more nervous than I am," he remarked, "and I'm always an old woman about these things. You're working too hard on this, Briscoe."

"I always work hard," Keith said. "I like it that way."

"And nights, too?"

"Nights, too."

"That's bad business. We're not as young as we used to be. There comes a time when we have to taper off a little." Gonzales pushed his hat back on his head and stretched his legs out in front of him giving the seat a tug backward. "At least that's what they tell me," he added, "but with five kids they don't tell me how. You've got kids, haven't you?"

Keith didn't answer. He looked for a cigarette in his pocket, but the package was empty. Down on the corner, just beyond the alleyway, he could see a drugstore. Drugstores carried cigarettes and no conversation about things he didn't care to discuss.

"I'm going for some smokes," he said. "Tell our friend not to peddle his towels until I get back."

The drugstore was on the same side of the street as the apartment house they were watching. Out of curiosity, he crossed over and walked past the front door. It was open to let in the air, but the hall was empty. He walked past the alley and on to the drugstore. He bought the cigarettes and walked back, still walking slowly because he was in no hurry to get back into that hot sedan. Gonzales was right: he was nervous. His hands trembled as he slit the tax stamp on the cigarette box. At the mouth of the alley he paused to light a cigarette, and then promptly forgot about it and let it fall to the ground.

A few minutes earlier, the alley had been deserted. Now a battered gray coupe was parked against the hedges about twenty feet back from the street. He looked up. The sidewalk in front of him was empty, but across the street Gonzales was climbing out of the sedan. Gonzales walked hurriedly toward the front door of the building, a man with his mind on his business. He didn't see Keith at all. The picture fell into place. Keith went directly to the coupe. It was an old

Chevvy, license number KUJ770. He stepped around to the door and looked for the card holder on the steering post. It had slipped out of focus, but the door was unlocked. When he opened the door, he saw something that had dropped to the floor of the car and was half hidden under the seat. It was dirty from being kicked about, but it was blue and it had a black French poodle on it. He dropped the towel to the floor and went to work on the card holder. The registration tab slid into view: George Kawalik, 1376¼ N. 3rd Street.

Keith had the whole story in his hand. Gonzales hadn't seen the coupe; he couldn't have seen it from the far side of the hedge. He stepped back, intending to go after Gonzales, and it was then that he heard the shot. He waited. There may have been a shout from within the building. He was never sure because what happened, when it did happen, happened very fast. He had started around the edge of the hedge when suddenly the hedge burst open to erupt a head—blond, close-cropped, a face—wild, contorted with fear—and then a body, long but bent almost double as it stumbled and fell forward toward the coupe. The door was wrenched open, and the face appeared above the steering wheel before Keith could orient himself for action. He was already at the curb twenty feet away from the car. He turned back just as the coupe leaped forward and was forced to scramble in fast retreat to avoid being run down. The retreat came to a sudden stop as he collided with about a hundred and eighty pounds of mobile power which turned out to be Gonzales.

"Was that him in the coupe? Did you see him?"

The coupe was a gray blur racing toward the corner.

"Did you see the car? Did you get the number?"

Gonzales had a right to shout. A killer had slipped through his fingers. A two-time murderer was getting away.

"That fool woman and her rattlesnake gun!"

Keith recovered his breath.

"Did she fire the shot?" he asked.

"No—but she had the gun in her hand when she opened the door. Clancy, inside, didn't catch her in time. The peddler saw it and ran for the back door. It was Clancy who fired. Did you get the license number?"

Gonzales's face was a big, sweaty mask in front of Keith's eyes. A big, homely, sweating face. A cop, a friend, a man in trouble. And Keith had the whole story on a tiny slip of paper in his hand.

He didn't hesitate.

"No," he said. "I didn't get it. I didn't have time."

Who could tell when decisions were made? An opportunity came, an answer was given—but that wasn't the time. Time was a fabric; the instant called now was only a thread. But it was done. The moment Keith spoke, he knew that something his mind had been planning all this time was already done. The fabric was already woven. He had only to follow the threads.

There was a murderer named George Kawalik who killed by pattern. He found an apartment where a woman lived alone. He watched the apartment, located the bedroom window, waited until Saturday when it was most likely he would find her home and made his scouting expedition under the pretext of peddling pretty towels. Sunday night was payoff night. He came, he stole, he killed.

There was another man named Keith Briscoe who had made a mistake. He didn't like to think about how or why he'd made it, but he had to think of a way out. He wasn't a young man any more. A little gray had begun to appear at his temples, and he was beginning to feel his limitations. It didn't seem fair that he had to pay for the rest of his life for a flirtation that had gone too far. It seemed less fair that his sons had no father, and that Faye was becoming a lonely woman who took her drinks stronger and who was running away to find the love he wanted to give her.

After leaving Gonzales, Keith had time to think about all these things. He sat alone in the furnished room and laid them out logically, mathematically in his mind. He put it into a simple formula: Keith plus Faye equalled home and happiness; Keith minus Elaine equalled Faye. The second part was no certainty, but it was at least a gamble and Keith not minus Elaine was no chance at all.

He knew the odds against murder. George Kawalik would be caught. He was no longer a footprint on the earth or a faceless shadow tall enough to reach up and slit a window screen, lean and agile enough to hoist himself into a room. He now had a face as well as a body; he had a method of operation; more important, he had a car. Gonzales had seen the gray coupe fleetingly, but he'd seen it with eyes trained to absorb details. And Gonzales had an organization to work with. Even as he sat thinking about it, Keith knew what forces were being put into operation. The coupe would be found. It might take days or even weeks, but it would be found. In the meantime, George Kawalik would kill again. That was inevitable. The compulsion that drove him to the act, whether it was a mental quirk or an addict's desperate need for money, would drive him again.

And Sunday was the night for murder.

On Saturday evening, as soon as it was dark, Keith went on an expedition. The address in Kawalik's registration slip wasn't easy to find in the dark; it wouldn't have been easy by daylight. It was a run-down, cluttered neighborhood ripe for a mass invasion of house movers. Old frame residences with the backyards cluttered by as many haphazard units as the building code would permit. Far to the rear of the lot he found Kawalik's number. The unit was dark and the shades drawn. He wanted to try the door, but it was too risky. This was no time to activate Kawalik's nervous trigger finger. He walked quietly around to the rear of the unit. All of the shades were drawn, but one window was open. He stood close to it for a few moments, and it seemed he could hear someone breathing inside. He moved on. The back door had an old-fashioned lock that any skeleton key would open. He fingered the key ring in his pocket and then decided to wait. He left the unit and walked back to the garages, a barracks-like row of open-front cubicles facing a narrow alley. The gray coupe was there.

Kawalik was holed in, the natural reaction to his narrow escape. That was good. Keith wasn't ready for him yet; he merely wanted to know where to find him at the proper time. He found his way back through the maze of units to the street, always with the uneasy knowledge that a crazed killer might be watching from behind those shaded windows. He'd almost reached the sidewalk when a voice out of the darkness brought him to a sudden halt.

"Looking for somebody, mister?"

A man's voice. Keith turned about slowly and then breathed easier. An old man stood in the lighted doorway of the front apartment. He had the suspicious eyes and possessive stance of a landlord protecting his property.

"I guess I had the wrong address," Keith said.

"What address you looking for?"

"A place to rent. A friend of mine told me he saw an empty unit here."

"Nothing to rent here," the old man answered.

"A unit with the shades rolled down," he said.

"That place's rented. The man rents it works nights."

Keith went home then. The old man still looked suspicious; Keith was satisfied.

There was only one thing to do before returning to Kawalik. In the morning, Keith called Elaine. It was nearly noon, but she sounded sleepy. Elaine's nights were unusually long. He'd worked out his story carefully. He was working late that night, he told her, but he had to see her. It was important. How about midnight? Elaine protested. Thelma was giving a party.

"Not another birthday?" he challenged.

She still protested. What did he want that couldn't wait? Freedom, he told her.

"And you know what I told you," she said.

"That it would cost me. Well, I may have a way of raising the fare. You don't dislike cash, do you?"

She fell for it. She would be home by midnight.

He watched the apartment from the street. At midnight all of the lights were blazing. At one o'clock the front lights went out, and he moved around to the rear. At one-thirty, the bedroom light went out. Elaine thought he'd stood her up and had gone to bed. She couldn't have made a bigger mistake.

Twenty minutes later, Keith entered Kawalik's apartment by way of the back door. The place was dark. For a few seconds, he was afraid Kawalik had more nerve than he'd been given credit for and was out calling on some other victim chosen in advance, but the fear left him when he reached the bedroom. A faint glow of moonlight penetrated the window blind outlining a long body under the sheet on the bed. Keith had his own gun in his hand. He switched on the flashlight. It was Kawalik, but he didn't stir. Keith moved closer to the bed. Kawalik's eyes were closed and his breathing heavy. One arm was thrown outside the sheet. Keith's first hunch had been correct. The arm was tattooed with needle marks and the last jolt must have been a big one. Kawalik wouldn't awaken for hours.

It was a better break than he'd bargained for. He played the flash around the room, not wanting to risk the lights because of the eagle-eyed landlord up front. Item by item, he found what he needed: Kawalik's .45 in a bureau drawer, a pair of canvas shoes with smooth rubber soles in the closet, a pair of gloves, a basketful of colored guest towels. Keith thumbed through the basket until he found a pink one. Shocking pink. It seemed appropriate for Elaine.

In the bathroom, he located the pocket knife among other interesting items: a hypodermic needle, a spoon with a fire-blackened bowl, the remnants of an old shirt torn in strips. One of the strips was stained with blood. Kawalik must have gone deeper than he intended locating the vein. Another blood-spotted strip dangled over the edge of the lavatory. He started to play the light downward and then switched it off instead. He didn't breathe again until he was convinced it was a cat he'd heard outside the building. He left the place then, without a light, locking the back door behind him.

Half an hour later, Keith climbed through Elaine's bedroom window. He was breathless and scared. A dozen times he'd expected her to hear him sawing away at the screen and ruin everything; but the other tenants of their building had always been thoughtful about such things as late, late television movies at full volume, or all-night parties of vibrant vocal range. This night was no exception and so Elaine would be sleeping, as usual, with ear plugs and eye mask. He really didn't need Kawalik's rubber-soled shoes on the deep-piled rug, but he did need Kawalik's signature—the pink towel to deposit in the linen closet in the bathroom. In the dressing room he found two purses in plain sight. He took the money from them, jamming the smaller, an evening bag in his pocket for subsequent deposit in the driveway below. That done, he went to the bed, leaned over Elaine and raised the eye mask. She awakened with a start, but she didn't scream. Elaine had nerve—nerve enough to stare at the shadowy figure standing over her bed until recognition came.

"Oh, it's you—"

And then she saw the gun in his hand. That was when Keith fired.

It was easy. Murder was easy. By the time he was safely in his car again, Keith was in the throes of an almost delirious elation. His nerves had been tauter than he knew; now they were unwinding with the power of a strong spring bursting its webbing. He knew how Kawalik felt when the shot in his bloodstream took effect: wild and free and about ten thousand feet up. Elaine was dead, and there wasn't a thing anyone could ever do to him. The noisy neighbors hadn't heard the shot, the evening bag had been dropped at the foot of the service ladder on the garage, the pink towel was in the linen closet and ballistics would match the bullet in Elaine's body to the two other bullets they were holding from two other identical crimes. And the beauty of it all was that Kawalik, when they caught him, wouldn't be able to remember but what he really had killed her. There was nothing left to do, but get the gun, gloves, shoes and the money back into Kawalik's apartment. After that, he belonged to the inevitable.

The inevitable was Sergeant Gonzales. Keith didn't see the police car in front of Kawalik's place until it was too late to drive on. He had slowed down to park, and Gonzales recognized him.

"I see you got my message," Gonzales called.

Keith shut off the motor. He had no idea how Gonzales had located Kawalik so quickly, but he could play dumb. Dumb meant silence.

"I told them at headquarters to call you just as I was leaving. It seemed a shame for you to miss out on the finish."

"The cat-killer?" Keith asked, his mind racing.

"We got him. I tell you, Briscoe, I've had an angel on my shoulder on this case. Another lucky break. The landlord here got suspicious. Said a fellow had been prowling around the place last night and heard somebody again, tonight, so he called the police. The boys didn't find a prowler, but out in the garage they found something more interesting—"

Keith's mind raced ahead of Gonzales's words. He wasn't ten thousand feet up any more, but he was still free. They'd have to look for the gun. He could help them do that; in the dark he could be a big help.

"—an old coupe," Gonzales added, "like the one they've been alerted for all day. They took a look. The front seat was full of blood."

In the dark he could help them find the gun and the gloves and the rubber-soled shoes—And then Keith's mind stopped racing and listened to Gonzales' words.

"Blood?" he echoed.

Blood, as on a strip of torn cloth in the bathroom. Blood,

as what was soaking into Elaine's bedclothes and beginning to stain Keith's hands.

Gonzales nodded.

"I guess Clancy's a better shot than we knew. The cat-killer won't climb tonight, Briscoe, or any other night. He's in there now so doped up he doesn't even know we've found him. It's a good way to kill the pain when somebody's blown a chunk out of your leg."

It wasn't really blood on Keith's hands; it was a gun. When he couldn't stand the weight of it any longer, he handed it to Gonzales. Gonzales would figure it out. A thread, a fabric, a pattern. Elaine had been right: he had a weakness, and a man with a weakness shouldn't play with guns.

WEIGHTY PROBLEM

by Duane Decker

Fatstuff could feel with his fingers that the material of the suit the nurse had brought him was corduroy. That meant it was not *his* suit.

"There has been a mistake," he said, in an annoyed voice. "These are not my clothes."

"That's true," she said. "But yours were badly ripped by your accident. These will have to do until you can buy others. Courtesy, by the way, of the Salvation Army."

"Oh!" Fatstuff said, mollified now. "And when will the bandages be removed from my eyes?"

"As soon as the doctor arrives," she explained. "And he's due quite soon."

"Good," he said. "I guess I'll wait and put the clothes on after I can see what I'm doing."

He leaned back against the upraised head of the hospital bed. He could remember his accident vividly. Late that morning he'd headed across the meadow behind Bertha's house. He knew what had been his undoing: he'd taken three stiff slugs of rye to build courage, then walked into a terribly hot sun. In his physically run-down condition that had been bad.

Far across the meadow, at the edge of the woods, he'd reached the dried-up well—the place where he'd hidden the money many weeks before. He had put the money inside a galvanized pail which was now resting on the dry bottom of the well.

In his hand he held a wire coat hanger with the triangular part flattened together so that it resembled a hook at the end of a long cucumber. At the top of the cucumber he had tied a length of cord. It formed a simple, home-made tool designed to be jockeyed back and forth below—until the hook managed to catch underneath the arched handle of the pail. Then Fatstuff could draw up the pail and remove the money —all thirty thousand of it.

But when he reached the well, the hot sun and the rye and his emaciated body had suddenly taken toll. Just before he fainted and blacked out, he remembered banging his head and body against the rough cement exterior of the well.

Now, glancing at the clock over the entrance to the hospital ward, Fatstuff saw it was almost five o'clock. That meant he had already lost six hours and that Bertha was no doubt pacing the bus station in Pomeroy, suspicion growing in her mind that he had skipped out on her with the money. If she got angry, vindictive—well, she could make a phone call and have the police come down on Fatstuff. He had to get out of here in a hurry, get the money and meet Bertha at the Pomeroy bus station before she ran out of patience.

He spoke to the nurse. "How did I get here in the first place?"

"A hunter happened to come along. He found you unconscious. And he half-carried you, half-dragged you to his car. That's how your clothes got ruined. Then he drove you here, to the emergency entrance."

Well, he could bless the hunter. He could think back so clearly—see how this whole thing had gone wrong from the start. Even though it still wasn't too late. The money was still there waiting for him—and only for him—to pick up.

The start of it had been all right. He'd been on the bum, hitchhiking his way to New York. Months ago. At dusk he'd found himself on the outskirts of this one-horse town, Appleton.

Farmhouse lights set back a hundred yards from the Post Road had cheerily beckoned him. Bertha answered his knock. She invited him in, asked him to dinner, suggested later that he stay over and get a good night's sleep. And he needed it.

Bertha, it developed, was a poor and lonely widow with nothing to her name except a termite-ridden farmhouse. Fatstuff, however, gladly stayed with her for a week. Then, once she trusted him, she told him of the scheme she'd worked out long ago, waiting for the right partner to come along.

She explained that up the Post Road, a quarter of a mile, there was a small dirt-road turnoff that led to only one place —the Macklin Tool Company. And every Friday at three, on the dot, old man Macklin drove past Bertha's house and took that dirt road turnoff—with the weekly payroll. He always did the job alone. A rugged individualist from way back. And he was old, feeble, trusting and defenseless.

All Fatstuff had to do, Bertha explained, was to be on that deserted dirt-road turnoff before three, then lie down in the middle of it when he heard the sound of the approaching car. Mr. Macklin, who was a deacon in the church, would stop his car and get out to offer help to a stricken man. And Bertha had an old Luger with which Fatstuff could menace Mr. Macklin while relieving him of the payroll. Meanwhile, she'd have left her old coupe hidden fifty yards up the Post Road, off to the side of the road. After getting the payroll, Fatstuff could hurry to the car and drive straight to the bus station in Pomeroy, take a bus to New York. Since no one had seen the car in connection with the holdup, Bertha would take the bus to Pomeroy, pick up her car and join Fatstuff in New York.

"It's as simple as that," Bertha said.

And Fatstuff had to agree. He went through with the plan.

The catch was, old man Macklin—it turned out—packed a gun. There had, subsequently, been an exchange of shots. But Fatstuff got there first with the most.

He left old man Macklin for dead—he looked dead to Fatstuff, who didn't waste too much time on an examination —and moved fast to Bertha's hidden coupe. But now, with a case of murder behind him, he didn't feel safe about driving to Pomeroy. Instead, he drove back to the farmhouse for refuge.

He knew he'd have to lie low for a while. That was why he thought of the idea of hiding the money in the dried-up well. As long as Bertha didn't know exactly where it was, she *had* to hide him and take care of him.

Later, on the radio, they heard that old man Macklin had died—but not before he had given a detailed and deadly accurate description of Fatstuff. "Fattest short man I ever did see," Macklin was quoted as saying. "One of those they call Mister Five-by-Five. Great big jowls on him. Thighs so thick they near split his pants when he moved. Great big stomach. You couldn't miss him. You'd pick him out of a big crowd."

Well, Fatstuff (and Bertha) realized it meant he couldn't show his face and body outside the farmhouse. In Appleton anybody at all would notice and remember. That was when he got the great idea: he'd move into the attic and diet himself into a scrawny, anemic little man.

He went to the attic and lived there in solitude for almost two months. She brought him nothing but lettuce, skim milk, grapefruit—things like that. The pounds evaporated until finally he had the look of a walking skeleton. Finally, he felt safe to make his move.

He turned on his side on the hospital bed. He was thinking that it had been the starvation diet as well as the slugs of rye and the hot sun that had caused him to faint at the well. But not knowing this, Bertha had taken the bus to Pomeroy and was waiting for him and if she got angry enough—

He said to the nurse, "Do I have to sign something to get out of here?"

"No," she said. "You're in good health now. And your mind is—well, the concussion was only temporary. Oh! Here's the doctor now!"

Fatstuff slid over so that he was sitting on the edge of the bed. He felt a touch on the shoulder as he heard the doctor's hearty voice say, "Hello!"

Fatstuff was feeling of the corduroy suit. "Doc," he said, "I sure appreciate the free clothes, but couldn't they have come a little closer on the fit?"

"I think you'll find they fit fairly well," the doctor said.

"Who's kidding who around here?" Fatstuff said. "This suit feels as big as a tent."

"Well, you've been quite a chowhound since your blackout."

"But—that was just this morning!"

He felt the doctor carefully removing the bandages from his eyes. He heard the doctor say, "Now *I* ask who's kidding who? This is September 17th. They brought you in here early in August. Your mind as well as your eyes have been pretty blank since then, since you hit that cement."

The bandages were off. Fatstuff stood up slowly. Then, with measured tread he advanced toward a full-length mirror he saw across the ward. He reached it, stared at himself in amazement. He couldn't stop staring.

Once more he was Mister Five-by-Five. Once more there were the enormous jowls, the heavy thighs, the enormous waist line. He was, if anything, more extraordinarily fat than he had been before that starvation diet. He knew the moment he set foot outside the hospital, he would be picked up by the police—before he could get the money or get out of town.

Behind him he heard the doctor say: "Well, are you ready to go now? You're free to go, you know."

He tried to find his voice, but all he could do was think, "No! No! No . . ."

WILLIE BETTS, BANKER

by Mike Brett

There are guys who get up in the morning at six o'clock, eat their breakfasts and go off to work and don't come home again until seven o'clock at night. They drive eight-year-old clunks, they work like horses, and at the end of the week their paychecks are gone as soon as they bring them home. Suckers, each and every one of them. But like they say, some guys got it and some guys ain't.

Me, I'm Willie Betts and I got it. I got it made, right down the line. I'm driving a brand-new car, equipped with air conditioning and leather custom-made seats, and I got a beautiful chick about twenty-five years younger than me for company while I drive to the West Coast.

She's a doll. Her name is Irma Taylor and she's got a terrific pair of legs and a real beautiful face and shape, a first-class dame.

Like I was saying, I'm not a guy who gets up in the morning and fights traffic to work. My suits are made to order and they cost me three hundred bucks, and they look it. I wear a diamond ring on the little finger of my right hand, and the stone is worth twelve grand. I wear custom-made shirts and the shoes on my feet cost fifty-five bucks.

I talk real quiet-like, you know what I mean. I don't like it when somebody talks loud. The only ones who talk loud like that are cheap punks. And I got no use for cheap punks and hoods. They don't know what class is. They wear flashy suits and loud ties and they look like gangsters. I can't stand the sight of them cheap punks.

A guy has got to look like what he is. I look like what I am. I'm the president of a bank. Yeah, that's right. I'm Willie Betts, banker.

I didn't get to be the president of a bank overnight. Nobody does. You got to work your way up to the top. But once you get there, it's great. You got money coming in all the time, and when you're the president of a bank, who's to stop you from taking money right off the top?

You got the dough and it gets you the dames, and the booze, and the fancy vacations, and the horses, and the big crap games. It's the good life.

Back in New York State they got a thing going called a State Investigation Commission and these guys and me, we don't see eye to eye on what I am.

I know I'm a banker.

They see it a different way. They call me a loan shark and a shylock. They call me and my associates—that's kind of a fancy name for my enforcers and collectors, but like I said, you got to have a touch of class—very uncooperative when we stand in back of the Fifth Amendment, on the grounds like we don't want to incriminate ourselves.

It's like these guys asking my associates all these questions are real stupid. What do they expect? They're going to ask my boys something and the answer is going to put my guys in stir. They'd be crazy if they thought my associates are going to talk.

Usurers they call me and my boys. They're crazy! They got to be crazy. Since when is a man who runs a legitimate business a usurer? They don't know what they're talking about. I'm a businessman and I work within the law. I got lawyers and accountants to tell me these things.

What they tell me, I got memorized, right in my head. I know it all, word by word. There are no restrictions on interest on loans above eight hundred dollars to individuals, or on loans of any amount to corporations. An interest rate of more than six percent annually on loans under eight hundred dollars to individuals is a misdemeanor, punishable by a maximum of one year in jail.

But that gives me a big laugh, because I don't put anything down on paper, so how is anybody going to know how much I'm collecting in vigorish? Vigorish, in case you don't know, is interest.

The law also says the extraction of any money by fear and force, even if it is owed, is considered extortion under state law, a felony punishable by a prison term of seven and a half to fifteen years.

But who's going to complain? One of the customers? He opens his mouth, we'll break his head and he knows it, too.

Like I say, I'm a banker. There ain't any two ways about

it. The State Investigation boys don't see it that way though.

In a way, I'm doing a big service to the community. Where else can a businessman or a guy who can't make the mortgage payments on his house go, after the bank turns him down as a bad risk? You keep a couple of tellers on the payroll and they tell you who's been turned down. That's right, they come to me. The vigorish starts at thirty percent, and it can go all the way up to a thousand percent, depending upon how the borrower pays the loan off. If he don't pay it, the vigorish goes up week by week. Some of my boys have collected two thousand dollars on a hundred-dollar loan.

But like I said, I'm doing the community a service.

There wouldn't have been any trouble, but one of the new guys made a bad mistake. He banged some borrower around, named Joe Teasdale, because Teasdale didn't want to pay the interest. Teasdale's wife called the cops when her old man had a heart attack and kicked off. The cops went after the guy who had banged him around and that's when the trouble started. He kept a complete set of books.

That was the rough part, because it was a small-time operation, small loans. This Teasdale guy had borrowed three hundred dollars. It's got hardly anything to do with the big operation I've got going for me now.

Like I was saying, I'm a banker now. This small-time loan thing is just a small part of the operation. Now I work hand in hand with some of the big banks. I can walk into a bank and walk out again with two million dollars in unsecured money. How many guys can do that?

Anyway, the newspapers got hold of the information in the books and they smeared it all over the front pages, the whole works, the amounts of the loans, the dates of payments of principal, and vigorish. Everybody started screaming and hollering. There was a great hullabaloo, and this stuff started with the State Investigation Commission.

I had a talk with my lawyer and he thought it would be a good idea for me to take a two-month trip and kind of disappear for a while, so I won't have to get up on the stand and claim the Fifth. I could have taken a flight to Europe or someplace, but there are always cops hanging around airports, and cops also hang out around railroad stations.

So my lawyer and myself both thought it was a good idea for me to take a tour of the country. The newspapers said that I was eluding a subpoena to the State Investigation hearings. That was true. I was. But the real reason that I didn't want to appear before any hearing, was that there was a chance that my picture could get into the newspapers. You never know when some creep is going to spot your face in the newspapers and point a finger at you. I got things going too good for anything like that to happen to me.

I didn't get to be the president of a banking firm overnight. I was a collector when I first started out. I broke some heads and some arms, and some guys who borrowed big and tried to run out wound up on the bottom of the Hudson River with thirty feet of chain wrapped around them to keep them there.

Like I was saying, I wear three-hundred-dollar suits and I drive new cars every year, and I got fancy dames for company. I'm a legitimate businessman. Of course, I got enforcers to collect. After all, you take a loan and you got to pay it back. If you think the vigorish it too high, then you don't come to me asking for money.

This investigating commission has got me marked lousy. They say I've bankrupted companies, corrupted bank officials, committed murder, and other acts of violence, and turned honest citizens into chattels of the mob. Those are very strong words and I don't like them words at all.

I see it a different way. I'm a legitimate banker and I expect to get paid. Of course, I'm not going to do any violence to anybody who can't pay me back. If you take money and don't pay it back, I won't break your head.

I'll have one of my boys do it for me. He'll break your head.

But in the meantime, I'm driving across the country and I figure I might as well enjoy myself. The scenery is very nice. Irma Taylor is very nice, too. She's a cute little doll with blonde hair that goes well with her suntanned arms. That was the nice part about taking a kid like her along. She looks like a kid, with that face of hers, but the white cotton dress she wears hangs on her real sweet. Irma's body don't look like no kid's.

She looks like a kid, but she'd been around plenty before I started to pay the rent. She'd belonged to one of my associates, but I knew that she was wasted on him, so I gave him the word and that was all there was to it. That's another advantage that comes with being the top man. All you got to do is say that you want something and you got it. You can do that if your name is Willie Betts.

I drove through Pennsylvania, Ohio, Indiana and Illinois. Then we cut south across Missouri. I think Irma first noticed the old jalopy in back of us in Illinois.

She had her shoes off and her feet propped up on the dash, and she said, "Willie, I think that old car is following us."

I saw him in the rearview mirror, a ten-year-old car. "Why do you say that?" I asked her.

"I seen him before, in Indiana."

"Don't mean anything," I said. "So what? There's a guy and he's going across Indiana and Illinois."

"Don't get sore, Willie. I just thought I'd tell you."

It didn't mean anything, but just the same I didn't like him on my tail like that. I didn't like him following me. When we got into Missouri, I got on the state highway and opened up. I left that old car eating my exhaust smoke. I lost him.

But outside of Bismarck, one of those deputy-sheriff guys wearing a ten-gallon hat waved me to a stop, and I knew it was bad, real bad. He'd want to see my driver's license, and if he had heard anything about a guy named Willie Betts back in the east, there'd be trouble.

Irma said, "Give me fifty bucks."

I dug into my pocket for it and handed it to her, while the deputy parked his car up ahead and walked back to us.

Irma wrinkled the fifty dollars up in her hand and got out of the car, and I could hear her talking to the deputy. I got an occasional drift of the conversation. She told him that we had just gotten married and I could hear her pouring it on heavy. I remembered she had come from this part of the country. And then she whispered something to the deputy that sounded like, "He's a rich old buzzard. Go on and take it."

I could see them both laughing. She shook his hand and I knew the money had passed hands. The deputy gave her a real friendly smile and then he drove off.

When she came back to the car, I was sweating like a horse. She climbed in and we took off. But I dropped back to the legitimate speed limit, and I kept it there all the way across Missouri and across Oklahoma and the top of Texas.

I spotted the guy in the jalop in back of me again, outside of Oklahoma City. I slowed, so that he pulled up and I got a good look at him and the car. He was a kid with a crew cut. I'd never seen him before. There wasn't any front license plate on his car.

But I wanted to find out what was going on, so when I came to the next traffic light and stopped, I jumped out of the car and walked back to where he stopped. And then, when I was almost there, the kid put the old car into reverse and backed down the street to a parked police car, and the kid began to talk to the cop. I didn't know what it was all about, maybe the kid was just asking directions, but I didn't want any part of it, so I got back into my car and took off.

The kid was in back of me all the way across Oklahoma. By now, Irma was half out of her head. She didn't take her eyes off the road in back of us even for a moment.

"He's back there, Willie," she'd keep saying. "There he is. I just saw him around that turn in the road."

I pulled over to the side of the road and stopped. He pulled off the road to the shoulder and stopped and waited some distance back.

I walked out to the middle of the road and started to yell, "Hey! What do you want?"

The kid just stayed in the old car.

I got back into my car and opened it up. We tore across the state of Texas at eighty-five miles an hour and I held it there. The windshield of the car became splattered with the bodies of hundreds of insects.

I didn't know what the creep wanted, but I wasn't going to stick around to find out. You never know, you take a young kid like that, and maybe he sees a new convertible and figures that the guy who's driving it is loaded, and so the kid decides to stick the guy up. And I don't carry a gun. I can't get a license to pack a gun in New York State because of my record.

I didn't care anything about being stopped by the cops for speeding. All I wanted was to get rid of the kid. All the way down to Lubbock I burned rubber.

There wasn't a sign of the old car when we stopped to eat supper at a diner. We were both feeling better. Somehow, the idea of the kid sticking to us that way was making a nervous wreck out of Irma. It frightened her and made her irritable. It bugged me, too.

Irma walked out to the car while I paid for the meal and

got some cigars. When I got out to the car, she wasn't in it. I heard a car pulling out of a parking space, real fast, and I caught one fast look at the jalopy tearing off down the highway. Irma was in it on the front seat beside the kid. In the light from the diner, I was able to make out that he had New York State license plates.

I started my car and gunned it, but stopped after twenty feet. One of the front shoes was flat. The kid must have let the air out of the tire.

I walked back to the diner and gave a kid two dollars to put the spare on for me. While he was changing the tire, I told him I wanted to go rabbit hunting tomorrow and I needed a shotgun.

I don't think I fooled the kid for a minute, but he had an old gun in his house he was willing to sell for thirty dollars. I drove him to his house and waited inside the car while he brought the gun and a box of shells out, and I paid him.

Then I took off toward New Mexico. I was going to find that kid with his old heap, and unless he gave me a good reason, that kid wasn't ever going to leave New Mexico. I had to cut my speed down when I came to Lovington, and then I saw him up ahead. There was one traffic light in town, and there was also a cop for those who didn't believe the light.

The jalopy moved ahead while I waited for the cop to signal me on. The kid was driving alone now, unless Irma was down on the floor, all trussed up. But I'm Willie Betts, and young punks don't give Willie Betts a rough time and get away with it. I didn't get to the top by being a nice guy.

I put the brights on when I got out of town. I went into a turn a little too fast and almost flipped over, so I cut back a little. I had the car under control when I hit the next turn doing about sixty, and that was when I spotted the log in the middle of the road. To the right of me, there was the face of a mountain; to the left, was what looked like a field in the darkness.

I turned the wheel to the left and stood on the power brakes. All four wheels locked. I went off the road and felt the front end give when I hit a ditch. My head hit the steering wheel, and I sat there for a while, trying to get rid of the dizzy feeling that overtook me.

Then there was a light shining in my eyes. The kid was there, outside the car.

I reached for the shotgun and I heard him say, "Hold it. Hold it, or I'll kill you."

I blinked and looked at the gun in his hand. The kid looked like he wasn't bluffing. "What do you want?" I asked.

"I want you," he said, and I thought I heard him laugh. "Get out of the car."

"What do you want? Why are you following me? Where's Irma?"

"Gone. Long since gone. I gave her a choice. I told her you'd had it, that you weren't going to the West Coast. She believed it. She got on the first bus that came along and took off. She doesn't want any part of what's happening out here. She doesn't want any part of this. She was very happy to get out of it in one piece. Come on, we go in my car from here on in."

"I ain't going anywhere with you," I said.

The kid reached in and shut the lights off on my car and pocketed the keys.

Out on the road, a big Diesel boomed into the turn and drove right on through.

The kid laughed. "The log is no longer there. My car is parked down the road about fifty feet. We're going to walk over to it and we're going to drive off. If you do as I tell you, nothing will happen to you. If you try anything, I'll kill you without giving it a second thought."

He held the gun on me and he stood very still. I believed him.

I drove his old car and he sat next to me and kept the gun on me. We drove over a rutted road that felt as though it was going to break every spring in the car. There was a full moon. I could see cactus plants, and in the distance I could make out the shapes of mountains. We drove along that broken road and we were the only car on it.

"We're in the Chihuahua Desert," the kid said.

"Who are you? What do you want?"

"I want you."

"What are you talking about? You crazy or something? Do you know who I am, you punk? I'm Willie Betts. You ever hear of Willie Betts?"

And then, so help me, this kid, this punk kid with the

crew cut, started to laugh. He said, "You think you're Willie Betts. But you're not Willie Betts."

"You're crazy."

"No," the kid said. "Not me. I'm not crazy, and you're not Willie Betts."

I was going to humor him, because the kid was a mental case. I could see that. "Yeah," I said. "I'm not Willie Betts. But who are you?"

He laughed. "You're not going to believe this, but I'm Willie Betts."

There wasn't any use in talking to the punk. He was just a wise-aleck little punk and if he didn't have that .32 aimed at my head, I'd kill him. The whole bit was some kind of crazy joke. I'm out in the middle of the desert with some kid who's off his rocker.

"Listen," I said. "Let's make some kind of a deal. There's got to be something you want, something, money, what do you want? Just name it."

"No. Money isn't any good out here."

The place where we stopped was a tiny stone hut and there was a heavy wooden door on it. He lighted the way with his flashlight and I watched him light a kerosene lantern.

"Take a look around," he said. "There's one window up high on the wall. My father built this place years ago, as a place where we could spend the summers. But what we had inside, we wanted to protect, so the place is made of stone and there are bars on the windows. You have enough kerosene to last you about three nights. After that, you stay here in darkness at night. But you can see the stars."

"Look kid, you're making some kind of real bad mistake. I never seen you before in my life. I'm Willie Betts. Let's go back to the car. We'll get into the first town and I'll wire for ten thousand bucks. That's money, kid, that's money."

"Keep your money."

"Then what do you want?"

"I'm going to give you a long rest."

"You trying to tell me you're going to kill me?"

"No. I don't want to kill you. There are blankets and a cot, and there's canned food in the closet."

The kid walked out, closed the door, and I heard him put a padlock on it.

The car door slammed shut. There was nothing else to do. I went to sleep on the cot.

I woke up at nine o'clock in the morning. The room was tiny and I went over every inch of it. I couldn't break the door down and the tiny window was barred. There wasn't any way for me to get out of this place.

It was crazy. I was dreaming the whole bit. How could something like this happen to Willie Betts? Who'd believe it? I would, because it was happening to me.

I brought the chair over to the window and by standing on it, I was able to look out. There was no sign of the car, but it could be on the other side of the shack. "Hey, kid!" I yelled. "Hey, kid!"

There wasn't any answer. I found a can of sardines, opened it, and ate them with some crackers. And then I started to look for water. There wasn't any, but the kid would be back with some. It figured.

I ate a can of tuna fish for supper. The next morning, I passed up another can of sardines. I was beginning to feel the lack of water, badly.

But I knew I had to eat. I had to keep my strength up. So when noon came around, I opened another can of tuna fish. I forced myself to walk around the little room for exercise. A guy could go crazy in this ten-by-ten shack unless he did something.

I was here two days, or was it three days? Four days?

There was a pencil in my pocket and I made marks on the wall. I had to know what day it was. I made four marks on the wall.

The kid came driving up on the fifth day. He stopped the car outside the shack and I climbed up on the chair and called to him. "Hey, I'm thirsty, kid. I'm really thirsty. Did you bring any water?"

I could see him climbing out of that old car and he was carrying a pail of water in all that dry, hot stillness out there. He stood outside the shack and I stared down at him. I knew he was crazy, because he kept swinging that pail of water.

"Come on," I said. "I'm thirsty. I've been without water."

I could see that little punk kid with his bucket full of water and I wanted to drink glassfuls of it.

"Open the door," I could hear a voice saying, and the voice didn't even sound like mine, because it was the voice of somebody begging. "Open the door and give me some of that water."

Then the kid with the crew cut looked up at me while I stared out of that little window. He took the pail in both hands and he pitched the water at me.

It was like it was happening in slow motion. I could see the water coming toward me. It was in a big mass, and then it hit the bars and my face and splashed into the room.

I cursed him, but all he did was turn his back and get back into the car. There was a dull pain in my forehead. It was almost a week now and I hadn't had any water, and all I had to eat was canned fish, which augmented my thirst.

But there was a little water on the rough wooden floor. I could see little puddles of it. I had to have water. I got down off the chair and on hands and knees, I placed my mouth to the dirty wooden floor and lapped.

Me, Willie Betts, was doing that! But nobody could see me, and I had to stay alive, because I had to kill that kid outside the shack.

I got back on the chair and I looked for the kid. He was standing near the car, grinning up at the window. "Hey, kid," I shouted. "What do you want? You name it. I'll give you fifty grand. I'm Willie Betts and I'm good for it. Fifty thousand dollars, and all you got to do is open the door and let me out."

The kid walked right up to the shack, then looked at me for a long time before he said anything. Then he said, "No, you're not Willie Betts," he said. "I'm Willie Betts."

That punk kid was pulling that stuff again. But I was wise to him. He was sick in the head. "Yeah," I said. "Okay. But who am I then?"

"You're Joe Teasdale," the kid said. "Remember, you had a heart attack when some guy roughed you up because you couldn't pay the eight hundred dollars, for the three hundred you borrowed to keep your kid in college."

I knew him then. He was Joe Teasdale's kid, the crew-cut college punk, and he was playing a game. He thought he was going to keep me locked up in a stone shack on the desert, with the bright, hot sun burning down on the shack until it broiled my brains.

But Willie Betts is too smart for a kid like that. I knew how to take care of that punk kid now, because I know what he's got on his mind. All I got to do is make him believe

I'm crazy, and that kid is going to come marching into the shack, and I'll get my hands on him, and I'm going to kill him.

But I was very tired now. I just wanted to lie down on the cot and stretch out and sleep. I was doing that all the time, taking naps now.

I was on the cot and I must have been asleep, because a noise woke me. It was late afternoon and there, in the window, was the kid. He was grinning at me. He must have been standing on something outside the window, maybe the car was next to the building.

He said, "Hello, Teasdale."

I didn't answer him.

Then he lifted a burlap sack to the window and dropped it into the shack. There was something moving in there, and before it hit the floor I saw the wriggling length of a snake coming out of the burlap sack.

It moved its full length out. I could see its triangular head, and I could see its tail shaking, and I could hear the rattling sound. I could see it looking at me, and I could see it begin to glide across the floor.

I grabbed the chair and swung it as the snake coiled, and I could see the lightning strike as it hit the bottom of the chair before I brought it down with all my strength, on that ugly, triangular-shaped head. The chair broke apart. The snake thrashed around for a while and finally stopped.

Then the face in the window was gone, and I could hear a man's voice screaming inside the room. I thought that was kind of strange, because I was the only guy there.

The kid dropped a half-filled canteen of water into the shack the next day. When I walked over to pick it off the floor, I heard him laugh, and he said, "Hey, Teasdale."

I looked up at him.

He had a burlap sack in his hands again. I could feel my heart pounding like it was going to explode. There was another rattlesnake in there! I knew it, and this time, maybe I wouldn't be so lucky.

He dropped the sack, and three desert rats came running out of it. Their feet made scratching noises on the wooden floor. I drank the water, but I couldn't sleep any more. Those rats would start gnawing at me if I went to sleep.

I fell asleep and a nightmare woke me. I dreamt one of

those rats had bitten my leg. In the darkness, I reached down and felt. I really had been bitten.

When light came into the shack in the morning, I took a piece of the splintered chair and went after the rats. They seemed to know what was coming, because they spread out, each of them moving to his own wall. They stared at me with their yellow eyes.

I cornered one, and killed him. Then the other two rushed me from either side, and I felt sharp teeth in my arm. I punched at him with my fist. And all the time I could hear somebody screaming in total terror, and I knew it was me.

Later, I lay panting on the cot. The room smelled of their blood and it was on me, too. I lost track of the days after that.

Then one day, I kind of fell against the door and it just swung open. The padlock was off. I was free, but I wasn't strong enough to walk too far. All I wanted was to get away from that stone shack. The kid wasn't anywhere around and the car was gone too.

A guy with a badge on his shirt, in a white car, stopped me when I made it to the highway. He took a look at me and his face paled. He said, "Get in the car, mister. We'll rush you over to the hospital."

And then he was playing a real funny game. He was blowing that siren of his just like he was a real cop. But I knew different. Anybody could see that he was just a fake cop.

"What's your name, mister?" he asked.

"I'm Joe Teasdale," I said. "That's me. Joe Teasdale."

I wasn't going to tell him about that crazy kid, that Willie Betts, who was dropping rattlesnakes and rats through the window. They'd think I was crazy.

BUS TO CHATTANOOGA

by Jonathan Craig

Janie June Hibbins was still sore from the strapping Uncle
Elmore had given her yesterday afternoon, and every so
often she would wince a little and shift her position in the
rocker. It was hard to sew by the light of the coal-oil lamp,
but she had had a lot of practice at it and she was within a
few stitches of finishing the white cotton dress she was
patterning on the one in the Sears Roebuck catalogue.

It wasn't as if she'd done anything wrong, she reflected
as she changed her position again. She hadn't. It was just that
there weren't enough hours in the day to do all the work
Uncle Elmore figured a healthy young girl ought to do. She
didn't know how much longer she could stand it. Ever since
Ma and Pa had died and Uncle Elmore had moved in, life
had been just plain miserable. Uncle Elmore had always been
one of the meanest men in the hills, and lately he had been
getting even meaner. It had got so that all she had to do
was look at him slant-wise, and he'd go for the strap.

"Mind you keep your eye on that whiskey still, missy,"
Uncle Elmore had ordered her just before he climbed in
his battered old car and started down the rutted road that
wound through the Smoky Mountains for almost ten miles
before it finally came out on the highway to Chattanooga.
"I want that mash cooked right and proper. If it ain't, I'll be
giving you a birthday present you won't like one little bit."

"Yes, sir, Uncle Elmore," Janie June had said.

"And don't be leaving the cabin after sundown. I don't
want no female kin of mine spooning around in the dark
with any of these young bucks around here. You hear me,
girl?"

"Yes, sir."

"You better remember it, too. Unless you crave a whup-
ping for a birthday present. How old will you be, anyhow?"

"Eighteen."

"Well, that ain't going to keep you from getting whupped. And being the prettiest girl on the mountain ain't going to keep you from it, neither. You just better learn to step a sight more lively, Janie June Hibbins."

"Oh, I will, Uncle Elmore."

"Fetch me a jar of 'shine. I plumb forgot."

Janie ran into the cabin, grabbed up one of the quart fruit jars she had just filled with corn whiskey, and rushed back to the car.

"Mind what I told you," Uncle Elmore called back as the car rattled off. "I don't keep that strap hanging on the wall just for show, you know."

Now, as Janie June took the last stitch in the hem of the dress and knotted the thread, she heard the banjo clock in the other room strike three. It was later than she'd thought, and she hurriedly hung up the dress and blew out the lamp and crossed to the window to watch for the bus to Chattanooga.

The bus came along up there on Piney Ridge at a few minutes after three, and on nights when Janie June was too troubled in her mind to sleep, she liked to watch for it and dream about how wonderful it would be if only she had enough money to run off to Chattanooga, where there weren't any Uncle Elmores, or smelly whiskey stills, or hard work from sun to sun, or strappings that left a girl so sore she could hardly sit down. There was a full moon tonight, and Piney Ridge was so bright that Janie June could see almost as well as if it were daytime.

Just beneath the crest of the ridge, straight across from the cabin, Janie June saw something which made her forget about the bus completely. There, on the abandoned road that led down from the ridge through Nuzum's Notch, a car was moving very slowly with its lights out. As she watched, the car halted by the mouth of the China River Cave, where she had played so often as a child, and two men got out. She could tell they were men, but no more than that. They moved quickly, their shadowy forms merging briefly with the larger shadow of the car before they separated from it again and started toward the cave. But now they were carrying something between them, something that looked very much like another man. They were swallowed by the black shadow at the mouth of the cave for a few moments; then the two of them came back alone, took what appeared to be a half-filled gunnysack from the car, and went back into the cave again. This time, they stayed inside much longer. When they came out, neither of them carried anything. They got into the car, still without having made a sound of any kind, and let the car coast down the road for a long way before they started the engine.

Janie June stared across the hollow at the black mouth of the cave, stark against the silver-gray of the moonwash on the surrounding rocks, for almost a full minute.

A person would be crazy to go up there, she told herself. A person would have to be touched, even to think about it.

She was still telling herself this as she went out to the other room, took down the lantern from the nail on the wall, picked up some matches from the box beside the cookstove, and set out for the cave.

She had been running up and down these hills all her life, and except for slowing down a little when she circled the grove where Uncle Elmore had his still, and which he had surrounded with trip-wires and deep, covered man-pits as a protection against revenue agents and Sheriff Orv Loonsey, she ran all way.

China River Cave—called that because, it was said, the small but rapid river inside it went all the way to China—wasn't much bigger than the cabin. Janie June lighted the lantern, set it on a rock, and looked about her.

There was nothing there. Janie June knew the cave as well as she knew her own room, and there was no place where even a half-filled gunnysack could have been hidden, much less a man's body. She picked up the lantern again and walked over to the edge of the underground river and stood looking down at the raging water. The river poured through the cave so fast that the water seemed to boil, and Janie June shuddered a little with the thought of what had happened to the man the other two had carried into the cave. The current would have sucked him out of sight in a second, and now the onrushing river would speed him through the bowels of the earth forever.

As Janie June turned away to leave, the lantern glinted on something in the dust just in front of her, and she picked it up. It was a narrow gold tie-clasp with the name *Duke* engraved on it in very small script. She studied it thoughtfully, and then threw it in the river. She wouldn't want anyone to know she'd seen *that*, because then they might suspect she'd seen a whole lot more. She put out the lantern and left the cave.

As she started down the slope, Janie June saw headlights on the road that led to the cabin. They were still a long way off, but they were coming fast. That would be Uncle Elmore's car, she knew, and if she meant to reach the cabin before he did, she'd really have to hurry. What he'd do if he found her gone was just too awful to think about.

It was a good thing her skirt was so short, she reflected as she ran across Froggy Bottom and started up the opposite slope toward the cabin; this was no time to be hampered. She ran faster than she ever had before, even in the daytime, and every time she came to one of Uncle Elmore's trip-wires or covered man-pits, she leaped right over it, rather than lose the time it would take to run around it. But still, she had to circle around in back of the cabin, to keep herself out of the headlights of the approaching car, and she reached her bedroom window only half a minute before the car pulled into the yard. By the time she'd climbed inside, Uncle Elmore and some other man were already stomping across the creaking planks of the front porch.

Then Uncle Elmore was hammering on her door. "Wake up in there," he yelled. He was drunk, she could tell. Real drunk.

"That you, Uncle Elmore?" she called, trying to make her voice sound as if she'd only just awakened.

"You know durn good and well who it is," Uncle Elmore said. "Get yourself on out here, girl. We got company."

Janie June waited about as long as it would have taken her to put on her dress, and then she went out into the other room.

"Breakfast," Uncle Elmore said as soon as she appeared. "And don't let the grass grow, neither." He was bald and toothless, but his shoulders and chest were enormous, and when he moved his arms, the bulging muscles writhed beneath the freckled skin like so many snakes. He was sitting at the table with another, much younger man, and right now he had that mean grin on his face, the one he always got when he was mighty pleased with himself. "Eggs and ham and grits and taters and some of them damson preserves," he said. "Stir your stumps, Janie June."

"Yes, sir, Uncle Elmore," Janie June said as she hurried over to the cookstove.

The young man sitting at the table with Uncle Elmore had dark hair and eyes and a small, neat mustache, and he was every bit as good-looking as Uncle Elmore was ugly. He smiled at Janie June and started to get to his feet.

Uncle Elmore laughed scornfully. "No need to get up for *her*," he said. "That's only Janie June. My niece."

"Good Lord," the man said softly.

"What in tarnation's wrong with you, Burt?" Uncle Elmore asked.

"You didn't tell me your niece was so pretty," Burt said.

"All it does is make her sassy," Uncle Elmore said.

"I never would have believed it," Burt said, staring at Janie June, occupied with her cooking.

"Hurry up with them victuals, girl," Uncle Elmore said as he turned on the old battery radio on the table. "I figure there just might be something interesting on the radio—eh, Burt?"

"Maybe so," Burt said. "My name's Burt Connor, Janie June."

"I'm right pleased to meet you," Janie June said.

Harsh and strident guitar music filled the room, and Uncle Elmore turned the radio down a little. "Fetch us a jar of 'shine, girl," he said.

Janie June took a jar of whiskey and two water glasses to the table and went back to the stove.

"You got a steady boyfriend, Janie June?" Burt asked.

"No, sir." Janie June said.

Uncle Elmore laughed. "You're growing calf eyes, I swear, Burt," he said, filling his glass. "You must've seen a girl or two *some* time or other."

"I've seen a lot of them," Burt said. "But I never saw one as—"

"Hush!" Uncle Elmore said, the glass halfway to his mouth. "Listen."

". . . and the Chattanooga police still have no leads in the robbery and abduction of notorious gambler Duke Mahannah," the voice on the radio was saying. "Informed sources, however, have revealed that Mahannah's wall safe, which his kidnapers apparently forced him to open, contained almost thirty thousand dollars. . . . And now your Nightowl Newscaster would like just a moment of your time to tell you about—"

Uncle Elmore switched off the radio, downed the entire

glass of moonshine in two long swallows, and winked at Burt.

"Well, now, what do you think of that?" he said. "Dang if it don't look like somebody's gone and stole that poor man's thirty thousand dollars." He shook his head and clucked his tongue. " 'Course, you can't believe everything you hear on the radio, now can you?"

Burt smiled, his eyes still on Janie June. "No," he said. "You sure can't." He drank some of his whiskey, coughed, and drank some more. "You make good liquor, Elmore."

"Well, thanks," Uncle Elmore said. "I take my pains with it. Janie June, what's slowing up them victuals?"

"Don't rush her," Burt said.

"I'll rush her with a strap," Uncle Elmore said.

"Oh, you wouldn't do that," Burt said, laughing.

"I wouldn't eh?" Uncle Elmore said, reaching for the fruit jar. "How about some more 'shine in that glass, Burt?"

"Thanks," Burt said. "I don't mind if I do."

"Too bad we ain't got anything to celebrate, eh, Burt?" Uncle Elmore said, grinning broadly.

Burt grinned, too. "Yes, isn't it?" he said.

"Hurry up with that food, girl," Uncle Elmore said.

"Yes, Uncle Elmore," Janie June said. "It's all ready." She filled two plates at the stove and carried them to the table. "Can I go back to bed now, Uncle Elmore?" she asked.

"Why not stay up with us a while?" Burt said. "You like to dance, Janie June?"

"Go on to bed," Uncle Elmore said. "I want you peart and lively tomorrow. You hear?"

"Yes, sir," Janie June said as she opened the door of her room. "I was real glad to meet you, Mr. Connor."

"The same," Burt said, smiling. "I'll be seeing you again, Janie June. In fact, I just might be seeing you a lot."

Janie June bolted the door behind her and lay down on her bed with her clothes on and listened to the voices in the other room. An hour crawled by as the voices grew thicker and sleepier and the silences came oftener and lasted longer. Then there was a silence that stretched on for several minutes, and finally Uncle Elmore began to snore. When Janie June tiptoed to the door and put her eye to the crack between it and the jamb, she saw that Uncle Elmore was asleep on his cot and Burt Connor was asleep at the table, his head resting on his forearm and his mouth slightly pursed, as if he were whistling.

Well, Janie June reflected as she crawled out the window, Uncle Elmore and Burt Connor wouldn't have thrown a bag of money in the river, the way they had poor Mr. Duke Mahannah's body, and that was for sure. She knew now what they'd done with the money—the only thing they *could* have done with it.

Twenty minutes later, the lantern beside her, Janie June was lying flat on her stomach beside the rushing water in the China River Cave, her arm in the water up to the elbow, feeling along the knobby surface of the undercut rock beneath her, probing for what she knew had to be there.

At last she found it—a taut wire tied to a fist-sized projection on the rock. The pull of the current on whatever was on the other end of the wire was so strong that the wire almost cut her fingers as she drew it up hand over hand, and if she hadn't been such a strong girl for her size she wouldn't have been able to pull it up at all.

It wasn't a gunnysack on the end of the wire, but a clear plastic bag as big as one, and it was more than half full of paper money.

Just as Janie June started to undo the wire from the gathered top of the bag, she thought she heard something. Her fingers seemed to freeze on the wire, and she crouched there, motionless, not even breathing. She heard it again —the sound of pebbles dislodged from the slope beneath the cave.

It had to be either Uncle Elmore or Burt Connor, she knew. Whoever it was, he'd kill her for sure. He'd know she knew what had happened to poor Mr. Duke Mahannah, and he'd kill her and throw her in the river.

She'd never thought so fast in her life. Whoever it was, he would already have seen the light of the lantern, so there was no use trying to do anything about that. But if he didn't already know who was in the cave, she still had a chance to keep from being caught.

That chance was to hide in the water. And since a wet dress would give her away later, she'd have to take it off. She dropped the bag of money back into the river, and then whipped the dress—which was all she had on—over her head and wedged it into the crevice between two rocks, where no one could see it. Then she slid into the water, and, making sure of each handhold before she trusted her life to it, worked herself back beneath the overhanging stone shelf of the river bank, just as she had done so many times in play when she was a little girl. Only her head and shoulders were above the hissing surface of the water now, and she hooked her fingers over a small ridge in the rock and fought the savage tow of the current that threatened to tear her hands loose at any second and send her hurtling through the earth for all eternity.

She heard the hollow pound of heavy boots in the cave, and then Uncle Elmore's surprised curse when he found no one there. Swearing to himself steadily, Uncle Elmore began to pull up the wire attached to the money bag. The bag broke through the surface of the water, and a moment later Janie June heard the soft plop as Uncle Elmore dropped it on the cave floor.

Uncle Elmore's swearing broke off abruptly. "Burt!" he said. "I didn't hear you come in."

"I didn't mean for you to," Burt Connor's voice said. His voice was flat and cold, not at all the way it had been back at the cabin. "Caught you red-handed, didn't I?"

"What the Sam Hill are you talking about?" Uncle Elmore demanded.

Burt's laugh was ugly. "I kind of figured on you double-crossing me, but I didn't think it'd be so soon."

"Listen here—" Uncle Elmore began. "Hey, now! What're you doing with that knife?"

"You're a dead man, Elmore," Burt said. "Did you know that?"

"You got me wrong, Burt," Uncle Elmore said, his voice breaking. "I wasn't going to take the money. I seen a light up here and I—"

"Stop lying," Burt said.

"Get away from me with that knife, Burt!" Uncle Elmore yelled. "Don't do it, Burt! Burt, listen to me, I swear I never—"

"Good-by, Elmore," Burt said, and then Uncle Elmore's body splashed into the water only a yard from Janie June's head, and in spite of herself, Janie June heard herself gasp.

The next instant, a big, hard hand had fastened on her wrist and was pulling her out of the water.

But when Burt had hauled her up beside him and saw that she was completely naked, he gaped at her in stunned disbelief and forgot for an instant to retain his viselike grip on her wrist. That instant was all Janie June needed to jerk away from him and dart for the mouth of the cave. Burt lunged after her, but his clutching hands slipped off her wet body and he could not hold her.

Down the slope she raced, with Burt just behind her. His legs were longer than hers, but she knew every foot of the way and he did not. If only she could reach the cabin before he caught her, she could grab the rifle from over the fireplace and keep him from killing her.

And then, just as she was almost halfway across Froggy Bottom, she slipped on the dew-slick grass and fell. She was up and running again almost at once, but now Burt was only a few steps behind her. As she started up the slope to the cabin, she cast a terrified glance over her shoulder and saw that he was even closer than she had thought, the knife in his hand flashing horribly in the moonlight. She'd never reach the cabin now, she knew; she was as good as dead this very second.

And then she remembered. The pits! The brush-covered man-pits around the grove where Uncle Elmore had his still!

The nearest pit was only a dozen yards away. She veered toward it, and at the last instant swerved to one side, hoping that Burt would crash through the thin layer of brush and fall into the deep pit below.

But it was not to be. Burt had changed his own course when he saw her change hers, and his pounding feet skirted the pit by inches.

He had her now for sure, Janie June knew. There wasn't any other pit she could lead him to without doubling back the way she had come. She could already imagine the knife sinking into her back, and she heard herself begin to whimper. She tried to run even faster.

Then she felt another sudden surge of hope, and she *did* run faster. She'd forgotten about the trip-wires. There was one in the ankle-deep grass thirty yards ahead. It was the last one between here and the cabin, and it would be the last chance she'd have to save her life.

She reached the trip-wire a heartbeat before Burt did, leaped over it, and sprinted on. Burt's foot caught on the wire and he went sprawling headlong, his body skidding across the wet grass to come to a sudden stop against a stump.

Janie June ran into the cabin, jerked the rifle off the wall, and ran back out. She'd just have to shoot Mr. Connor, she guessed; there didn't seem to be any other way to keep him from killing her.

Burt Connor lay completely still, and as Janie June cautiously approached him, she saw that his neck was bent at an odd angle and that his eyes were wide open, staring at nothing. He was dead, she realized; the fall had broken his neck.

Janie June stood looking down at him for a long moment, and then she took a deep breath and let it out very slowly. She would have to put Mr. Connor's body in the river, and that was going to be an awful chore. She wouldn't have any trouble getting it down the slope to Froggy Bottom, of course, and towing it across the slippery grass in the hollow wouldn't be too hard, either. But pulling it up the far slope to the cave was going to be mighty tiring work.

Three hours later, when Janie June waved down the bus on top of Piney Ridge and climbed aboard, she was wearing her new white cotton dress and carrying Uncle Elmore's scuffed, twine-bound cardboard suitcase.

She found an empty seat, put the suitcase on her lap, and sat smiling out the window as the big bus roared back to life and started off down the mountain on its way to Chattanooga.

"Look how tight that girl's holding on to that old wreck of a suitcase," she heard a woman across the aisle whisper. "You'd think she had a fortune in there."

THE FEEL OF THE TRIGGER

by Donald E. Westlake

Abraham Levine, detective of Brooklyn's Forty-third Precinct, sat at a desk in the squadroom and worriedly listened to his heart skip every eighth beat. It was two o'clock on Sunday morning, and he had the sports section of the Sunday *Times* open on the desk, but he wasn't reading it. He hadn't been reading it for about ten minutes now. Instead, he'd been listening to his heart.

A few months ago, he'd discovered the way to listen to his heart without anybody knowing he was doing it. He'd put his right elbow on the desk and press the heel of his right hand to his ear, hard enough to cut out all outside sound. At first it would sound like underwater that way, and then gradually he would become aware of a regular clicking sound. It wasn't a beating or a thumping or anything like that, it was a click-click-click-click—click-click-

There it was again. Nine beats before the skip that time. It fluctuated between every eighth beat and every twelfth beat. The doctor had told him not to worry about that, lots of people had it, but that didn't exactly reassure him. Lots of people died of heart attacks, too. Lots of people around the age of fifty-three.

"Abe? Don't you feel good?"

Levine guiltily lowered his hand. He looked over at his shift partner, Jack Crawley, sitting with the *Times* crossword puzzle at another desk. "No, I'm okay," he said. "I was just thinking."

"About your heart?"

Levine wanted to say no, but he couldn't. Jack knew him too well.

Crawley got to his feet, stretching, a big bulky harness bull. "You're a hypochondriac, Abe," he said. "You're a good guy, but you got an obsession."

"You're right." He grinned sheepishly. "I almost wish the phone would ring."

Crawley mangled a cigarette out of the pack. "You went to the doctor, didn't you? A couple of months ago. And what did he tell you?"

"He said I had nothing to worry about," Levine admitted. "My blood pressure is a little high, that's all." He didn't want to talk about the skipping.

"So there you are," said Crawley reasonably. "You're still on duty, aren't you? If you had a bum heart, they'd retire you, right?"

"Right."

"So relax. And don't hope for the phone to ring. This is a quiet Saturday night. I've been waiting for this one for years."

The Saturday night graveyard shift—Sunday morning, actually, midnight till eight—was usually the busiest shift in the week. Saturday night was the time when normal people got violent, and violent people got murderous, the time when precinct plainclothesmen were usually kept on the jump.

Tonight was unusual. Here it was, after two o'clock, and only one call so far, a bar holdup over on 23rd. Rizzo and McFarlane were still out on that one, leaving Crawley and Levine to mind the store and read the *Times*.

Crawley now went back to the crossword puzzle, and Levine made an honest effort to read the sports section. Levine was a short and stocky man, fifty-three years of age. In his plain brown baggy suit he looked chunky, flabbier than he really was. His face was round and soft, with mild eyes and a formless nose and a broad sensitive mouth, all bracketed by faint fine lines like a pencil sketch.

They read in silence for ten minutes, and then the phone rang on Crawley's desk. Crawley scooped the receiver up to his ear, announced himself, and listened.

The conversation was brief. Crawley's end of it was limited to yesses and got-its, and Levine waited, watching his wrestler's face, trying to read there what the call was about.

Then Crawley broke the connection by depressing the cradle buttons, and said, over his shoulder, "Holdup. Grocery store at Green and Tanahee. Owner shot. That was the beat cop, Wills."

Levine got heavily to his feet and crossed the squadroom

to the coatrack, while Crawley dialed a number and said, "Emergency, please."

Levine shrugged into his coat, purposely not listening to Crawley's half of the conversation. It was brief enough, anyway. When Crawley came over to get his own coat, he said, "DOA. Four bullets in him. One of these trigger-happy amateurs."

"Any witnesses?"

"Wife. The beat man—Wills—says she thinks she recognized the guy."

"Widow," said Levine.

Crawley said, "What?"

Widow. Not wife any more, widow. "Nothing," said Levine.

If you're a man fifty-three years of age, there's a statistical chance your heart will stop this year. But there's no sense getting worried about it. There's an even better statistical chance that it *won't* stop this year. So, if you go to the doctor and he says don't worry, then you shouldn't worry. Don't think morbid thoughts. Don't think about death all the time, think about life. Think about your work, for instance.

But what if it so happens that your work, as often as not, is death? What if you're a precinct detective, the one the wife calls when her husband just keeled over at the breakfast table, the one the hotel calls for the guest who never woke up this morning? What if the short end of the statistics is the end you most often see?

Levine sat in the squad car next to Crawley, who was driving, and looked out at the Brooklyn streets, trying to distract his mind. At two A.M. Brooklyn is dull, with red neon signs and grimy windows in narrow streets. Levine wished he'd taken the wheel.

They reached the intersection of Tanahee and Green, and Crawley parked in a bus-stop zone. They got out of the car.

The store wasn't exactly on the corner. It was two doors down Green, on the southeast side, occupying the ground floor of a red-brick tenement building. The plate-glass window was filthy, filled with show-boxes of Kellogg's Pep and Tide and Premium Saltines. Inevitable, the letters SALADA were curved across the glass. The flap of the rolled-up green awning above the window had lettering on it, too: "Fine Tailoring."

There were two slate steps up, and then the store. The glass in the door was so covered with cigarette and soft-drink decals it was almost impossible to see inside. On the reverse, they all said, "Thank you—call again."

The door was closed now, and locked. Levine caught a glimpse of blue uniform through the decals, and rapped softly on the door. The young patrolman, Wills, recognized him and pulled the door open. "Stanton's with her," he said. "In back." He meant the patrolman from the prowl car parked now out front.

Crawley said, "You got any details yet?"

"On what happened," said Wills, "yes."

Levine closed and locked the door again, and turned to listen. This was their method, his and Crawley's, and it made them a good team. Crawley asked the questions, and Levine listened to the answers.

"There weren't any customers," Wills was saying. "The store stays open till three in the morning, weekends. Midnight during the week. It was just the old couple—Kosofsky, Nathan and Emma—they take turns, and they both work when it's busy. The husband—Nathan—he was out here, and his wife was in back, making a pot of tea. She heard the bell over the door—"

"Bell?" Levine turned and looked up at the top of the door. There hadn't been any bell sound when they'd come in just now.

"The guy ripped it off the wall on his way out."

Levine nodded. He could see the exposed wood where screws had been dragged out. Somebody tall, then, over six foot. Somebody strong, and nervous, too.

"She heard the bell," said Wills, "and then, a couple minutes later, she heard the shots. So she came running out, and saw this guy at the cash register—"

"She saw him," said Crawley.

"Yeah, sure. But I'll get to that in a minute. Anyway, he took a shot at her, too, but he missed. And she fell flat on her face, expecting the next bullet to get her, but he didn't fire again."

"He thought the first one did it," said Crawley.

"I don't know," said Wills. "He wasted four on the old guy."

"He hadn't expected both of them," said Levine. "She rattled him. Did he clean the register?"

"All the bills and a handful of quarters. She figures about sixty-two bucks."

"What about identification?" asked Crawley. "She saw him, right?"

"Right. But you know this kind of neighborhood. At first, she said she recognized him. Then she thought it over, and now she says she was mistaken."

Crawley made a sour sound and said, "Does she know the old man is dead?"

Wills looked surprised. "I didn't know it myself. He was alive when the ambulance got him."

"Died on the way to the hospital. Okay, let's go talk to her."

Oh, God, thought Levine. *We've got to be the ones to tell her.*

Don't think morbid thoughts. Think about life. Think about your work.

Wills stayed in front, by the door. Crawley led the way back. It was a typical slum-neighborhood grocery. The store area was too narrow to begin with, both sides lined with shelves. A glass-faced enamel-sided cooler, full of cold cuts and potato salad and quarter-pound bricks of butter, ran parallel to the side shelves down the middle of the store. At one end there was a small ragged-wood counter holding the cash register and candy jars and a tilted stack of English-muffin packages. Beyond this counter were the bread and pastry shelves and, at the far end, a small frozen-food chest. This row gave enough room on the customer's side for a man to turn around, if he did so carefully, and just enough room on the owner's side for a man to sidle along sideways.

Crawley led the way down the length of the store and through the dim doorway at the rear. They went through a tiny dark stock area and another doorway to the smallest and most overcrowded living room Levine had ever seen.

Mohair and tassels and gilt and lion's legs, that was the living room. Chubby hassocks and overstuffed chairs and amber lampshades and tiny intricate doilies on every flat surface. The carpet design was twists and corkscrews, in muted dark faded colors. The wallpaper was somber, with a curling ensnarled vine pattern writhing on it. The ceiling was low. This wasn't a room, it was a warm crowded den, a little hole in the ground for frightened gray mice.

The woman sat deep within one of the overstuffed chairs.

She was short and very stout, dressed in dark clothing nearly the same dull hue as the chair, so that only her pale frightened face was at first noticeable, and then the heavy pale hands twisting in her lap.

Stanton, the other uniformed patrolman, rose from the sofa, saying to the woman, "These men are detectives. They'll want to talk to you a little. Try to remember about the boy, will you? You know we won't let anything happen to you."

Crawley asked him, "The lab been here yet?"

"No, sir, not yet."

"You and Wills stick around up front till they show."

"Right." He excused himself as he edged around Levine and left.

Crawley took Stanton's former place on the sofa, and Levine worked his way among the hassocks and drum tables to the chair most distant from the light, off to the woman's left.

Crawley said, "Mrs. Kosofsky, we want to get the man who did this. We don't want to let him do it again, to somebody else."

The woman didn't move, didn't speak. Her gaze remained fixed on Crawley's lips.

Crawley said, "You told the patrolman you could identify the man who did it."

After a long second of silence, the woman trembled, shivered as though suddenly cold. She shook her head heavily from side to side, saying, "No. No, I was wrong. It was very fast, too fast. I couldn't see him good."

Levine sighed and shifted position. He knew it was useless. She wouldn't tell them anything, she would only withdraw deeper and deeper into the burrow, wanting no revenge, no return, nothing but to be left alone.

"You saw him," said Crawley, his voice loud and harsh. "You're afraid he'll get you if you talk to us, is that it?"

The woman's head was shaking again, and she repeated, "No. No. No."

"He shot a gun at you," Crawley reminded her. "Don't you want us to get him for that?"

"No. No."

"Don't you want us to get your money back?"

"No. No." She wasn't listening to Crawley, she was merely shaking her head and repeating the one word over and over again.

"Don't you want us to get the man who killed your husband?"

Levine started. He'd known that was what Crawley was leading up to, but it still shocked him. The viciousness of it cut into him, but he knew it was the only way they'd get any information from her, to hit her with the death of her husband just as hard as they could.

The woman continued to shake her head a few seconds longer, and then stopped abruptly, staring full at Crawley for the first time. "What you say?"

"The man who murdered your husband," said Crawley. "Don't you want us to get him for murdering your husband?"

"Nathan?"

"He's dead."

"No," she said, more forcefully than before, and half-rose from the chair.

"He died in the ambulance," said Crawley doggedly, "died before he got to the hospital."

Then they waited. Levine bit down hard on his lower lip, hard enough to bring blood. He knew Crawley was right, it was the only possible way. But Levine couldn't have done it. To think of death was terrible enough. To *use* death—to use the fact of it as a weapon—no, that he could never do.

The woman fell back into the seat, and her face was suddenly stark and clear in every detail. Rounded brow and narrow nose and prominent cheekbones and small chin, all covered by skin as white as candle wax, stretched taut across the skull.

Crawley took a deep breath. "He murdered your husband," he said. "Do you want him to go free?"

In the silence now they could hear vague distant sounds, people walking, talking to one another, listening to the radio or watching television, far away in another world.

At last, she spoke. "Brodek," she said. Her voice was flat. She stared at the opposite wall. "Danny Brodek. From the next block down."

"A boy?"

"Sixteen, seventeen."

Crawley would have asked more, but Levine got to his feet and said, "Thank you, Mrs. Kosofsky."

She closed her eyes.

In the phone book in the front of the store they found one

Brodek—Harry R—listed with an address on Tanahee. They went out to the car and drove slowly down the next block to the building they wanted. A taxi passed them, its vacancy light lit. Nothing else moved.

This block, like the one before it and the one after it, was lined on both sides with red brick tenements, five stories high. The building they were looking for was two thirds of the way down the block. They left the car and went inside.

In the hall, there was the smell of food. The hall was amber tile, and the doors were dark green, with metal numbers. The stairs led up abruptly to the left, midway down the hall. Opposite them were the mailboxes, warped from too much rifling.

They found the name, shakily capital-lettered on an odd scrap of paper and stuck into the mailbox marked 4-D.

Above the first floor, the walls were plaster, painted a green slightly darker than the doors. Sounds of television filtered through most of the doors. Crawley waited at the fourth floor landing for Levine to catch up. Levine climbed stairs slowly, afraid of being short of breath. When he was short of breath, the skipped heart beats became more frequent.

Crawley rapped on the door marked 4-D. Television sounds came through this one, too. After a minute, the door opened a crack, as far as it would go with the chain attached. A woman glared out at them. "What you want?"

"Police," said Crawley. "Open the door."

"What you want?" she asked again.

"Open up," said Crawley impatiently.

Levine took out his wallet, flipped it open to show the badge pinned to the ID label. "We want to talk to you for a minute," he said, trying to make his voice as gentle as possible.

The woman hesitated, then shut the door and they heard the clinking of the chain being removed. She opened the door again, releasing into the hall a smell of beer and vegetable soup. She said, "All right. Come." Turning away, she waddled down an unlit corridor toward the living room.

This room was furnished much like the den behind the grocery store, but the effect was different. It was a somewhat larger room, dominated by a blue plastic television set with a bulging screen. An automobile chase was careening across the screen, prewar Fords and Mercuries, accompanied by frantic music.

A short heavy man in T-shirt and work pants and slippers sat on the sofa, holding a can of beer and watching the television set. Beyond him, a taller, younger version of himself, in khaki slacks and flannel shirt with the collar turned up, was watching, with a cold and wary eye, the entrance of the two policemen.

The man turned sourly, and his wife said, "They're police. They want to talk to us."

Crawley walked across the room and stood in front of the boy. "You Danny Brodek?"

"So what?"

"Get on your feet."

"Why should I?"

Before Crawley could answer, Mrs. Brodek stepped between him and her son, saying rapidly, "What you want Danny for? He ain't done nothing. He's been right here all night long."

Levine, who had waited by the corridor doorway, shook his head grimly. This was going to be just as bad as the scene with Mrs. Kosofsky. Maybe worse.

Crawley said, "He told you to say that? Did he tell you why? Did he tell you what he did tonight?"

It was the father who answered. "He didn't do nothing. You make a federal case out of everything, you cops. Kids maybe steal a hubcap, knock out a streetlight, what the hell? They're kids."

Over Mrs. Brodek's shoulder, Crawley said to the boy, "Didn't you tell them, Danny?"

"Tell them what?"

"Do you want me to tell them?"

"I don't know what you're talking about."

On the television screen, the automobile chase was finished. A snarling character said, "I don't know what you're talking about." Another character said back, "You know what I'm talking about, kid."

Crawley turned to Mr. Brodek. "Your boy didn't steal any hubcap tonight," he said. "He held up the grocery store in the next block. Kosofsky's."

The boy said, "You're nuts."

Mrs. Brodek said, "Not Danny. Danny wouldn't do nothing like that."

"He shot the old man," said Crawley heavily. "Shot him four times."

"Shot him!" cried Brodek. "How? Where's he going to get a gun? Answer me that, where's a young kid like that going to get a gun?"

Levine spoke up for the first time. "We don't know where they get them, Mr. Brodek," he said. "All we know is they get them. And then they use them."

"I'll tell you where when he tells us," said Crawley.

Mrs. Brodek said again, "Danny wouldn't do nothing like that. You've got it wrong."

Levine said, "Wait, Jack," to his partner. To Mrs. Brodek, he said, "Danny did it. There isn't any question. If there was a question, we wouldn't arrest him."

"The hell with that!" cried Brodek. "I know about you cops, you got these arrest quotas. You got to look good, you got to make a lot of arrests."

"If we make a lot of wrong arrests," Levine told him, trying to be patient for the sake of what this would do to Brodek when he finally had to admit the truth, "we embarrass the Police Department. If we make a lot of wrong arrests, we don't stay on the force."

Crawley said, angrily, "Danny, you aren't doing yourself any favors. And you aren't doing your parents any favors either. You want them charged with accessory? The old man died!"

In the silence, Levine said softly, "We have a witness, Mrs. Brodek, Mr. Brodek. The wife, the old man's wife. She was in the apartment behind the store and heard the shots. She ran out to the front and saw Danny at the cash register. She'll make a positive identification."

"Sure she will," said the boy.

Levine looked at him. "You killed her husband, boy. She'll identify you."

"So why didn't I bump her while I was at it?"

"You tried," said Crawley. "You fired one shot, saw her fall, and then you ran."

The boy grinned. "Yeah, that's a dandy. Think it'll hold up in court? An excitable old woman, she only saw this guy for a couple of seconds, while he's shooting at her, and then he ran out. Some positive identification."

"They teach bad law on television, boy," said Levine. "It'll hold up."

"Not if I was here all night, and I was. Wasn't I, Mom?"

Defiantly, Mrs. Brodek said, "Danny didn't leave this room for a minute tonight. Not a minute."

Levine said, "Mrs. Brodek, he *killed*. Your son took a man's life. He was seen."

"She could have been mistaken. It all happened so fast, I bet she could have been mistaken. She only thought it was Danny."

"If it happened to your husband, Mrs. Brodek, would *you* make a mistake?"

Mr. Brodek said, "You don't make me believe that. I know my son. You got this wrong somewhere."

Crawley said, "Hidden in his bedroom, or hidden somewhere nearby, there's sixty-two dollars, most of it in bills, three or four dollars in quarters. And the gun's probably with it."

"That's what he committed murder for, Mr. Brodek," said Levine. "Sixty-two dollars."

"I'm going to go get it," said Crawley, turning toward the door on the other side of the living room.

Brodek jumped up, shouting, "The hell you are! Let's see your warrant! I got that much law from television, mister, you don't just come busting in here and make a search. You got to have a warrant."

Crawley looked at Levine in disgust and frustration, and Levine knew what he was thinking. The simple thing to do would be to go ahead and make the arrest and leave the Brodeks still telling their lie. That would be the simple thing to do, but it would also be the wrong thing to do. If the Brodeks were still maintaining the lie once Crawley and Levine left, they would be stuck with it. They wouldn't dare admit the truth after that, not even if they could be made to believe it.

They must be wondering already, but could not admit their doubts. If they were left alone now, they would make the search themselves that they had just kept Crawley from making, and they would find the money and the gun. The money and the gun would be somewhere in Danny Brodek's bedroom. The money stuffed into the toe of a shoe in the closet, maybe. The gun under the mattress or at the bottom of a full wastebasket.

If the Brodeks found the money and the gun, and believed that they didn't dare change their story, they would get rid of the evidence. The paper money ripped up and flushed down the toilet. The quarters spent, or thrown out the window. The gun dropped down a sewer.

Without the money, without the gun, without breaking Danny Brodek's alibi, he had a better than even chance of getting away scot-free. In all probability, the grand jury wouldn't even return an indictment. The unsupported statement of an old woman, who only had a few hectic seconds for identification, against a total lack of evidence and a rock solid alibi by the boy's parents, and the case was foredoomed.

But Danny Brodek had *killed*. He had taken life, and he couldn't get away with it. Nothing else in the world, so far as Levine was concerned, was as heinous, as vicious, as *evil*, as the untimely taking of life.

Couldn't the boy himself understand what he'd done? Nathan Kosofsky was dead. He didn't exist any more. He didn't breathe, he didn't see or hear or taste or touch or smell. The pit that yawned so widely in Levine's fears had been opened for Nathan Kosofsky and he had tumbled in. Never to live, ever again.

If the boy couldn't understand the enormity of what he'd done, if he was too young, if life to him was still too natural and inevitable a gift, then surely his parents were old enough to understand. Did Mr. Brodek never lie awake in bed and wonder at the frail and transient sound of his own heart pumping the life through his veins? Had Mrs. Brodek not felt the cringing closeness of the fear of death when she was about to give birth to her son? They knew, they had to know, what murder really meant.

He wanted to ask them, or to remind them, but the awful truths swirling in his brain wouldn't solidify into words and sentences. There is no real way to phrase an emotion.

Crawley, across the room, sighed heavily and said, "Okay. You'll set your own parents up for the bad one. That's okay. We've got the eye-witness. And there'll be more; a fingerprint on the cash register, somebody who saw you run out of the store—"

No one had seen Danny Brodek run from the store. Looking at the smug young face, Levine knew there would be no fingerprints on the cash register. It's just as easy to knuckle the No Sale key to open the cash drawer.

He said, to the boy's father, "On the way out of the store, Danny was mad and scared and nervous. He pulled the door open, and the bell over it rang. He took out his anger and his nervousness on it, yanking the bell down. We'll find that somewhere between here and the store, and there may be prints on it. There also may be scratches on his hand, from yanking the bell mechanism off the door frame."

Quickly, Danny said, "Lots of people got scratches on their hands. I was playing with a cat this afternoon, coming home from school. He give me a couple scratches. See?" He held out his right hand, with three pink ragged tears across the surface of the palm.

Crawley said, "I've played with cats, too, kid. I always got my scratches on the back of my hand."

The boy shrugged. The statement needed no answer.

Crawley went on, "You played with this cat a long while, huh? Long enough to get three scratches, is that it?"

"That's it. Prove different."

"Let's see the scratches on your left hand."

The boy allowed tension to show for just an instant, before he said, "I don't have any on my left hand. Just the right. So what?"

Crawley turned to the father. "Does that sound right to you?"

"Why not?" demanded Brodek defensively. "You play with a cat, maybe you only use one hand. You trying to railroad my son because of some cat scratches?"

This wasn't the way to do it, and Levine knew it. Little corroborative proofs, they weren't enough. They could add weight to an already held conviction, that's all they could do. They couldn't change an opposite conviction.

The Brodeks had to be reminded, some way, of the enormity of what their son had done. Levine wished he could open his brain for them like a book, so they could look in and read it there. They must know, they must at their ages have some inkling of the monstrousness of death. But they had to be reminded.

There was one way to do it. Levine knew the way, and shrank from it. It was as necessary as Crawley's brutality with the old woman in the back of the store. Just as necessary. But more brutal. And he had flinched away from that earlier, lesser brutality, telling himself *he* could never do such a thing.

He looked over at his partner, hoping Crawley would think of the way, hoping Crawley would take the action

from Levine. But Crawley was still parading his little corroborative proofs, before an audience not yet prepared to
accept them.

Levine shook his head, and took a deep breath, and stepped
forward an additional pace into the room. He said, "May I
use your phone?"

They all looked at him, Crawley puzzled, the boy wary,
the parents hostile. The father finally shrugged and said,
"Why not? On the stand there, by the TV."

"May I turn the volume down?"

"Turn the damn thing off if you want. Who can pay any
attention to it?"

"Thank you."

Levine switched off the television set, then searched in
the phone book and found the number of Kosofsky's Grocery. He dialed, and a male voice answered on the first ring,
saying, "Kosofsky's. Hello?"

"Is this Stanton?"

"No, Wills. Who's this?"

"Detective Levine. I was down there a little while ago."

"Oh, sure. What can I do for you, sir?"

"How's Mrs. Kosofsky now?"

"How is she? I don't know. I mean, she isn't hysterical
or anything. She's just sitting there."

"Is she capable of going for a walk?"

Wills', "I guess so," was drowned out by Mr. Brodek's
shouted, "What the hell are you up to?"

Into the phone, Levine said, "Hold on a second." He
cupped his hand over the mouthpiece, and looked at the
angry father. "I want you to understand," he told him, "just
what it was your son did tonight. I want to make sure you
understand. So I'm going to have Mrs. Kosofsky come up
here. For her to look at Danny again. And for you to look
at her while she's looking at him."

Brodek paled slightly, and an uncertain look came into
his eyes. He glanced quickly at his son, then even more
quickly back at Levine. "The hell with you," he said defiantly. "Danny was here all night. Do whatever the hell you
want."

Mrs. Brodek started to speak, but cut it off at the outset,
making only a tiny sound in her throat. But it was enough
to make the rest swivel their heads and look at her. Her eyes
were wide. Strain lines had deepened around her mouth, and

one hand trembled at the base of her throat. She stared in mute appeal at Levine, her eyes clearly saying, *Don't make me know*.

Levine forced himself to turn away, say into the phone, "I'm at the Brodeks. Bring Mrs. Kosofsky up here, will you? It's the next block down to your right, 1342, apartment 4-D."

It was a long silent wait. No one spoke at all from the time Levine hung up the telephone till the time Wills arrived with Mrs. Kosofsky. The five of them sat in the drab living room, avoiding one another's eyes. From another room, deeper in the apartment, a clock that had before been unnoticeable now ticked loudly. The ticks were very fast, but the minutes they clocked off crept slowly by.

When the rapping finally came at the hall door, they all jumped. Mrs. Brodek turned her hopeless eyes toward Levine again, but he looked away, at his partner. Crawley lumbered to his feet and out of the room, down the corridor to the front door. Those in the room heard him open the door, heard the murmur of male voices, and then the clear frightened voice of the old woman: "Who lives here? Who lives in this place?"

Levine looked up and saw that Danny Brodek was watching him, eyes hard and cold, face set in lines of bitter hatred. Levine held his gaze, pitying him, until Danny looked away, mouth twisting in an expression of scorn that didn't quite come off.

Then Crawley came back into the room, stepping aside for the old woman to follow him in. Beyond her could be seen the pale young face of the patrolman, Wills.

She saw Levine first. Her eyes were frightened and bewildered. Her fingers plucked at a button of the long black coat she now wore over her dress. In the brighter light of this room, she looked older, weaker, more helpless.

She looked second at Mrs. Brodek, whose expression was as terrified as her own, and then she saw Danny.

She cried out, a high-pitched failing whimper, and turned hurriedly away, pushing against Wills, jabbering, "Away! Away! I go away!"

Levine's voice sounded over her hysteria: "It's okay, Wills. Help her back to the store." He couldn't keep the bitter rage from his voice. The others might have thought it was rage against Danny Brodek, but they would have been wrong. It was rage against himself. What good would it do to convict Danny Brodek, to jail him for twenty or thirty years? Would it undo what he had done? Would it restore her husband to Mrs. Kosofsky? It wouldn't. But nothing less could excuse the vicious thing he had just done to her.

Faltering, nearly whispering, Mrs. Brodek said, "I want to talk to Danny. I want to talk to my son."

Her husband glared warningly at her. "Esther, he was here all—"

"I want to talk to my son!"

Levine said, "All right." Down the corridor, the door snicked shut behind Wills and the old woman.

Mrs. Brodek said, "Alone. In his bedroom."

Levine looked at Crawley, who shrugged and said, "Three minutes. Then we come in."

The boy said, "Mom, what's there to talk about?"

"I want to talk to you," she told him icily. "Now."

She led the way from the room, Danny Brodek following her reluctantly, pausing to throw back one poisonous glance at Levine before shutting the connecting door.

Brodek cleared his throat, looking uncertainly at the two detectives. "Well," he said. "Well. She really—she really thinks it was him, don't she?"

"She sure does," said Crawley.

Brodek shook his head slowly. "Not Danny," he said, but he was talking to himself.

Then they heard Mrs. Brodek cry out from the bedroom, and a muffled thump. All three men dashed across the living room, Crawley reaching the door first and throwing it open, leading the way down the short hall to the second door and running inside. Levine followed him, and Brodek, grunting, "My God. Oh, my God," came in third.

Mrs. Brodek sat hunched on the floor of the tiny bedroom, arms folded on the seat of an unpainted kitchen chair. A bright-colored shirt was hung askew on the back of the chair.

She looked up as they ran in, and her face was a blank, drained of all emotion and all life and all personality. In a voice as toneless and blank as her face, she told him, "He went up the fire escape. He got the gun, from under his mattress. He went up the fire escape."

Brodek started toward the open window, but Crawley pulled him back, saying, "He might be waiting up there. He'll fire at the first head he sees."

Levine had found a comic book and a small gray cap on the dresser top. He twisted the comic book in a large cylinder, stuck the cap on top of it, held it slowly and cautiously out the window. From above, silhouetted, it would look like a head and neck.

The shot rang loud from above, and the comic book was jerked from Levine's hand. He pulled his hand back and Crawley said, "The stairs."

Levine followed his partner back out of the bedroom. The last he saw in there, Mr. Brodek was reaching down, with an awkward shyness, to touch his wife's cheek.

This was the top floor of the building. After this, the staircase went up one more flight, ending at a metal-faced door which opened onto the roof. Crawley led the way, his small flat pistol now in his hand, and Levine climbed more slowly after him.

He got midway up the flight before Crawley pushed open the door, stepped cautiously out onto the roof, and the single shot snapped out. Crawley doubled suddenly, stepping involuntarily back, and would have fallen backward down the stairs if Levine hadn't reached him in time and struggled him to a half-sitting position, wedged between the top step and the wall.

Crawley's face was gray, his mouth strained white. "From the right," he said, his voice low and bitter. "Down low. I saw the flash."

"Where?" Levine asked him. "Where did he get you?"

"Leg. Right leg, high up. Just the fat, I think."

From outside, they could hear a man's voice braying, "Danny! Danny! For God's sake, Danny!" It was Mr. Brodek, shouting up from the bedroom window.

"Get the light," whispered Crawley.

Not until then had Levine realized how rattled he'd been just now. Twenty-four years on the force. When did you become a professional? How?

He straightened up, reaching up to the bare bulb in its socket high on the wall near the door. The bulb burned his fingers, but it took only the one turn to put it out.

Light still filtered up from the floor below, but no longer enough to keep him from making out shapes on the roof. He crouched over Crawley, blinking until his eyes got used to the darkness.

To the right, curving over the top of the knee-high wall around the roof, were the top bars of the fire escape. Black shadow at the base of the wall, all around. The boy was low, lying prone against the wall in the darkness, where he couldn't be seen.

"I can see the fire escape from here," muttered Crawley. "I've got him boxed. Go on down to the car and call for help."

"Right," said Levine.

He had just turned away when Crawley grabbed his arm. "No. Listen!"

He listened. Soft scrapings, outside and to the right. A sudden flurry of footsteps, running, receding.

"Over the roofs!" cried Crawley. *"Damn* this leg! Go after him!"

"Ambulance," said Levine.

"Go *after* him! *They* can make the call." He motioned at the foot of the stairs, and Levine, turning saw down there anxious, frightened, bewildered faces peering up, bodies clothed in robes and slippers.

"Go on!" cried Crawley.

Levine moved, jumping out onto the roof in a half-crouch, ducking away to the right. The revolver was in his hand, his eyes were staring into the darkness.

Three rooftops away, he saw the flash of white, the boy's shirt. Levine ran after him.

Across the first roof, he ran with mouth open, but his throat dried and constricted, and across the second roof he ran with his mouth shut, trying to swallow. But he couldn't get enough air in through his nostrils, and after that he alternated, mouth open and mouth closed, looking like a frantic fish, running like a comic fat man, clambering over the intervening knee-high walls with painful slowness.

There were seven rooftops to the corner, and the corner building was only three stories high. The boy hesitated, dashed one way and then the other, and Levine was catching up. Then the boy turned, fired wildly at him, and raced to the fire escape. He was young and lithe, slender. His legs went over the side, his body slid down; the last thing Levine saw of him was the white face.

Two more roofs. Levine stumbled across them, and he no longer needed the heel of his hand to his ear in order to hear his heart. He could hear it plainly, over the rush of his breathing, a brushlike throb—throb—throb—throb—throb—

Every six or seven beats.

He got to the fire escape, winded, and looked over. Five flights down, a long dizzying way, to the blackness of the bottom. He saw a flash of the boy in motion, two flights down. "Stop!" he cried, knowing it was useless.

He climbed over onto the rungs, heavy and cumbersome. His revolver clanged against the top rung as he descended and, as if in answer, the boy's gun clanged against metal down below.

The first flight down was a metal ladder, and after that narrow steep metal staircases with a landing at every floor. He plummeted down, never quite on balance, the boy always two flights ahead.

At the second floor, he paused, looked over the side, saw the boy drop lightly to the ground, turn back toward the building, heard the grate of door hinges not used to opening.

The basement. And the flashlight was in the glove compartment of the squad car. Crawley had a pencil flash, six buildings and three floors away.

Levine moved again, hurrying as fast as before. At the bottom, there was a jump. He hung by his hands, the revolver digging into his palm, and dropped, feeling it hard in his ankles.

The back of the building was dark, with a darker rectangle in it, and fire flashed in that rectangle. Something tugged at Levine's sleeve, at the elbow. He ducked to the right, ran forward, and was in the basement.

Ahead of him, something toppled over with a wooden crash, and the boy cursed. Levine used the noise to move deeper into the basement, to the right, so he couldn't be outlined against the doorway, which was a gray hole now in a world suddenly black. He came up against a wall, rough brick and bits of plaster, and stopped, breathing hard, trying to breathe silently and to listen.

He wanted to listen for sounds of the boy, but the rhythmic pounding of his heart was too loud, too pervasive. He had to hear it out first, to count it, and to know that now it was skipping every sixth beat. His breath burned in his lungs, a metal band was constricted about his chest, his head felt hot and heavy and fuzzy. There were blue sparks at the corners of his vision.

There was another clatter from deeper inside the basement, to the left, and the faint sound of a doorknob being turned, turned back, turned again.

Levine cleared his throat. When he spoke, he expected his voice to be high-pitched, but it wasn't. It was as deep and as strong as normal, maybe even a little deeper and a little louder. "It's locked, Danny," he said. "Give it up. Throw the gun out the doorway."

The reply was another fire flash, and an echoing thunderclap, too loud for the small bare-walled room they were in. And, after it, the whining ricochet as the bullet went wide.

That's the third time, thought Levine. *The third time he's given me a target, and I haven't shot at him. I could have shot at the flash, this time or the last. I could have shot at him on the roof, when he stood still just before going down the fire escape.*

Aloud, he said, "That won't do you any good, Danny. You can't hit a voice. Give it up, prowl cars are converging here from all over Brooklyn."

"I'll be long gone," said the sudden voice, and it was surprisingly close, surprisingly loud.

"You can't get out the door without me seeing you," Levine told him. "Give it up."

"I can see you, cop," said the young voice. "You can't see me, but I can see you."

Levine knew it was a lie. Otherwise, the boy would have shot him down before this. He said, "It won't go so bad for you, Danny, if you give up now. You're young, you'll get a lighter sentence. How old are you? Sixteen, isn't it?"

"I'm going to gun you down, cop," said the boy's voice. It seemed to be closer, moving to Levine's right. The boy was trying to get behind him, get Levine between himself and the doorway, so he'd have a silhouette to aim at.

Levine slid cautiously along the wall, feeling his way. "You aren't going to gun anybody down," he said into the darkness. "Not anybody else."

Another flash, another thunderclap, and the shatter of glass behind him. The voice said, "You don't even have a gun on you."

"I don't shoot at shadows, Danny. Or old men."

"*I* do, old man."

How old is he? wondered Levine. *Sixteen, probably. Thirty-seven years younger than me.*

"You're afraid," taunted the voice, weaving closer. "You ought to run, cop, but you're afraid."

I am, thought Levine. *I am, but not for the reason you think.*

It was true. From the minute he'd ducked into this basement room, Levine had stopped being afraid of his own death at the hands of this boy. He was fifty-three years of age. If anything was going to get him tonight it was going to be that heart of his, skipping now on number five. It wasn't going to be the boy, except indirectly, because of the heart.

But he *was* afraid. He was afraid of the revolver in his own hand, the feel of the trigger, and the knowledge that he had let three chances go by. He was afraid of his job, because his job said he was supposed to bring this boy down. Kill him or wound him, but bring him down.

Thirty-seven years. That was what separated them, thirty-seven years of life. Why should it be up to *him* to steal those thirty-seven years from this boy? Why should *he* have to be the one?

"You're a goner, cop," said the voice. "You're a dead man. I'm coming in on you."

It didn't matter what Danny Brodek had done. It didn't matter about Nathan Kosofsky, who was dead. An eye for an eye, a life for a life. No! A destroyed life could not be restored by more destruction of life.

I can't do it, Levine thought. *I can't do it to him.*

He said, "Danny, you're wrong. Listen to me, for God's sake, you're wrong."

"You better run, cop," crooned the voice. "You better hurry."

Levine heard the boy, soft slow sounds closer to his left, weaving slowly nearer. "I don't *want* to kill you, Danny!" he cried. "Can't you understand that? I don't *want* to kill you!"

"I want to kill *you,* cop," whispered the voice.

"Don't you know what dying is?" pleaded Levine. He had his hand out now in a begging gesture, though the boy couldn't see him. "Don't you know what it means to die? To stop, like a watch. Never to see anything any more, never to hear or touch or know anything any more. Never to *be* any more."

"That's the way it's going to be, cop," soothed the young voice. Very close now, very close.

He was too young. Levine knew it, knew the boy was too young to *feel* what death really is. He was too young to know what he wanted to take from Levine, what Levine didn't want to take from him.

Every fourth beat.

Thirty-seven years.

"You're a dead man, cop," breathed the young voice, directly in front of him.

And light dazzled them both.

It all happened so fast. One second, they were doing their dance of death here together, alone, just the two of them in all the world. The next second, the flashlight beam hit them both, the clumsy uniformed patrolman was standing in the doorway saying, "Hey!" Making himself a target, and the boy, slender, turning like a snake, his eyes glinting in the light, the gun swinging around at the light and the figure behind the light.

Levine's heart stopped, one beat.

And every muscle, every nerve, every *bone* in his body tensed and tightened and drew in on itself, squeezing him shut, and the sound of the revolver going off slammed into him, pounding his stomach.

The boy screamed, hurtling down out of the light, the gun clattering away from his fingers.

"Jesus God have mercy!" breathed the patrolman. It was Wills. He came on in, unsteadily, the flashlight trembling in his hand as he pointed its beam at the boy crumpled on the floor.

Levine looked down at himself and saw the thin trail of blue-gray smoke rising up from the barrel of his revolver. Saw his hands still tensed shut into claws, into fists, the first finger of his right hand still squeezing the trigger back against its guard.

He willed his hands open, and the revolver fell to the floor.

Wills went down on one knee beside the boy. After a minute, he straightened, saying, "Dead. Right through the heart, I guess."

Levine sagged against the wall. His mouth hung open. He couldn't seem to close it.

Wills said, "What's the matter? You okay?"

With an effort, Levine nodded his head. "I'm okay," he said. "Call in. Go on, call in."

"Well. I'll be right back."

Wills left, and Levine looked down at the new young death. His eyes saw the colors of the floor, the walls, the clothing on the corpse. His shoulders felt the weight of his overcoat. His ears heard the receding footsteps of the young patrolman. His nose smelled the sharp tang of recent gunfire. His mouth tasted the briny after-effect of fear.

"I'm sorry," he whispered.

CAPTIVE AUDIENCE

by Jack Ritchie

Adam Carlson listened to the faint howl of a dog, and fifteen seconds later he heard the hum of an airplane. The sound of the motors grew rapidly louder until the plane passed directly over the house.

In the glare of the naked overhead bulb, he glanced at his watch. 2:32 A.M.

Adam sat up on the cot and stared about the room once again. Twelve feet by fourteen. No windows. Solid concrete block construction except for the heavy oak door. Almost soundproof, but not quite. The dog must be fairly near.

How long had he been here? It seemed like days, but actually it had been only about eight hours. It had begun yesterday evening. Where would it end?

Adam had just put his car into the garage and begun the walk up the long path to the house when they stepped out of the darkness. There had been two of them, both hooded, and they held guns.

He had been startled, of course, but not really frightened. His hands had gone above his head. "Take the money, but leave the wallet." He had been thinking about the nuisance of getting duplicates of his driver's license and various other cards and identifications if the wallet were taken.

But they hadn't been concerned about his wallet or the money. The tall heavy-set man had merely indicated with the automatic that he wanted Adam to walk ahead of them.

They had gone back down the driveway, past the two gate posts, and to the dark sedan parked by the side of the gravel road.

Adam had been blindfolded and bound and put on the floor in the rear of the car. At first he had tried to keep track of the direction in which they drove. But they had turned again and again until he had become confused and given up.

After an hour the car had stopped and the ropes had been

removed from his ankles. With the blindfold still on, he had been led along a path and he had heard a door being opened. He had been guided down a flight of stairs and into this room.

When they untied his hands and removed the blindfold, he had blinked at the sudden light. As his eyes adjusted he had seen the bare room with its cot, its single chair, its table, and the pen and paper.

The big man had spoken for the first time. "Sit down," he ordered. "You're going to write a note to your wife. We're asking for two hundred thousand dollars."

Adam had stared at the hooded figures. "Two hundred thousand dollars?"

Perhaps there had been a smile behind the hood. "That's right, mister. Maybe you got it figured out by now why we picked you up."

Adam had licked his lips. "My wife left for Europe last week with her mother."

The two hooded men had looked at each other. Did they seem uncertain? The big man had raised the gun. "We want the two hundred thousand. We don't care how you get it or who gets it for you, but we want it."

Adam had sat down at the table. "Harold Bannister. He's my lawyer and long-time counselor."

The gun moved again. "Pick up the pen. I'll tell you what words to use."

And Adam had written:

> Dear Harold:
>   I want you to get two hundred thousand dollars to-gether, none of it in bills larger than one-hundreds.
>   You will be phoned instructions about what to do with it later.
>   Do not notify the police. If you do, you will never see me alive again.
>   ADAM CARLSON

The big man had read the note and then nodded. He and his partner had left the room and Adam had heard the heavy door being locked.

Now Adam lay down on the cot once again. He closed his eyes against the glare of the single bare bulb overhead.

Would they kill him after they got the money? But if that

was their intention, why would they bother to wear hoods? Adam grasped at that. As long as they wore the hoods—as long as they took the pains to make sure that he could not identify them later—his life was safe.

Adam woke with a start as he heard a key in the door. He glanced at his watch. Eight-twenty-five. He'd managed to fall asleep. He felt his heart pounding as he watched the door open.

The big man entered alone with a tray. And he was still hooded. "Your breakfast," he said.

He waited until Adam indicated that he'd eaten as much as he wanted and then took the blindfold out of his pocket. "You're going to phone your office. Tell your secretary that you won't be in for at least a week. Tell her you're taking a trip."

He was led to a spot just outside the door.

"What's your number?" the big man asked.

Adam told him and then heard the dialing. He felt the phone thrust into his hand. His secretary, Madge, answered the rings. "Madge," Adam said, "I won't be in for about a week. I'm taking a little vacation trip."

"Yes, sir," she said. "Where can I reach you in case I have to?"

"You won't have to," Adam said. "Just put everything off. Cancel all my appointments."

The big man took the phone from him. "Maybe there's somebody else you ought to call, too? Just remember, for your own health we wouldn't want anybody getting worried about you and telling the police."

Adam thought for a moment. "My housekeeper." He gave the big man his number and the phone was once again put into his hand.

"Mrs. Regan?"

"Yes," she said. "Is that you, Mr. Carlson?"

"Yes."

"Where are you? This morning when you didn't come down for breakfast, I got worried. I sent James looking for you, but he couldn't find you. He said that you must have come home last night though, because all the cars are in the garage."

"I did," Adam said. "But I left again early this morning. A friend of mine picked me up at the gate." He took a breath. "Mrs. Regan, I won't be home for about a week. Just taking sort of a vacation."

"All right," she said. "But a letter from your wife came in yesterday afternoon's mail. I left it on the hall table, but I guess you missed it."

"Yes," Adam said. "I guess I did."

"You'll want to pick it up before you go, won't you?"

"No. Just keep it until I get back."

There was a slight pause. "I could send it on to where you're staying?"

"No," Adam said, "I don't know exactly where that will be. I'll be on the road most of the time."

The big man led him back into the room and removed the blindfold. In the evening, his partner brought Adam supper.

They probably take turns guarding the door, Adam thought; the big man during the day and the little man during the night.

Adam spoke. "Have you heard anything from Bannister yet?"

The small man shook his head. He waited for Adam to eat. Impatiently, it seemed. He had the habit of pinching the knuckles of his right hand.

In the morning, the big man brought Adam breakfast.

Adam first sipped some coffee. "Have . . . have you gotten the money yet?"

The big man shook his head. "No. We're giving Bannister until Thursday."

The hours, the days, and the nights passed slowly. And then on Thursday afternoon when the big man entered the room, his voice was harsh. "Bannister's stalling." He removed the blindfold from his pocket. "I'm going to let you talk to him and you'd better be convincing. Tell him to have the money by noon tomorrow or he can forget about the whole thing. Do you understand what I mean?"

Adam wiped perspiration from his hands. "Yes. I understand."

At the phone, Adam waited until he got Bannister and then said, "Harold, why haven't you got the money?"

"Adam?" Bannister said. "Is that you?"

"Yes."

"Are you all right?"

"Yes," Adam said. "I'm all right. But they say that you're stalling."

Bannister hesitated. "No, Adam. But getting that much cash takes a little time. And I've been thinking, your Altiline Chemicals is at 28½ now. I thought that if we could wait until just Monday there might be an upturn."

"Sell it," Adam snapped. "Right now."

Bannister sighed. "All right, Adam. And about your share in the Shore Apartments, the best offer I can get now is $75,000 from Rogers."

"Let him have it." Adam gripped the phone. "Harold, you've got to have the money by noon tomorrow. If you don't have it by then, it will be too late."

The line was silent for five seconds. "I understand, Adam. I'll get it together somehow. You can count on me."

At one the next afternoon when the big man brought him his lunch, Adam rose from the cot. "Did Bannister get the money?"

The big man grunted. "We phoned and he says he has. But we'll find out for sure when we make the pickup tonight." He put the tray on the table. "Better pray that nothing goes wrong."

It was past ten that evening when Adam heard the key in the door lock. He found his heart pounding. Both of the men entered and they were still hooded.

Ten minutes later Adam found himself once again bound and blindfolded and lying in the back of a car. It seemed to him that they drove endlessly, but at last the car stopped. He was dragged out and thrown on the grass beside the road.

Adam waited, stiff with dread at what might happen in the next moment. Then he heard the car drive away.

He lay there for a minute breathing deeply with relief and then began working at his bonds. When he was free, he stood up. The night was bright with a full moon and half a mile down the country road he could make out the dark shape of a farmhouse and a barn. He began walking toward them to ask for help.

It was after two in the morning before the police finished questioning Adam. When he was released, he found Harold Bannister waiting.

Bannister looked tired. "The police have been at me,

Adam. Claim I should have reported the kidnapping to them when I got your note."

Outside the building, they got into Bannister's car. Adam rubbed his eyes. He was weary, but still too tense for sleep. "I could stand a drink."

Bannister turned the ignition key. "There's probably nothing open at this hour, but you can try one of my martinis."

Twenty minutes later, in Bannister's living room, Adam sat down in an easy chair and tried to relax. Bannister went to the liquor cabinet. "The one who phoned me had a Midwestern accent. Definitely a Midwestern accent. What about the other one?"

"I don't know," Adam said. "I never heard him say a word."

Then Adam heard the howling of the dog.

He stiffened as he caught the sound of the approaching plane. The noise grew and grew until the plane roared overhead.

Adam looked at his watch. 2:32 A.M.

His eyes widened. He had heard the dog and that airplane at the same time every night since Monday.

At the liquor cabinet, Bannister surveyed the bottles. "Now where the devil is that vermouth?" Absently he pinched the knuckles of his right hand.

"Ah," he said. "Here it is." He picked up the bottle and turned. "Well, let's hope that the police catch up with your kidnappers."

Adam had been staring at the floor, almost seeing the small room that must be in the basement. Now he looked up at the small lawyer. He smiled faintly. "Yes," he said. "I have a feeling they will."

ROOM TO LET

by Hal Ellson

Rain spattered the sill of the window where she stood, her gray eyes angry and her chin outthrust. Forlorn drops sounded a dirge beyond the curtain and glass; she didn't hear it, didn't notice the dreary street dropping swiftly toward the river. They were carrying the stretcher down the high stoop without trouble, for the dead man weighed no more than a stick.

The bloody bugger cheated me, thought Mrs. Flynn, her gaze on the gray blanket. *Not a cent to his name and owing me for his room.* She shook her head and watched the stretcher slide into the morgue-wagon, the door slam, attendant and driver in black gleaming raincoats wave to the policeman standing by and climb into the wagon. As the "wagon" drove off, the policeman glanced up at the house and walked away, head thrust against the wind of the wild March day.

"Well, that's that," said Mrs. Flynn aloud, turning from the window and hustling on her short fat legs for the hall door. Only one flight to the empty room above, but she was wheezing through her pinched nostrils when she reached it. The door was still ajar, the room brackish with shadow, silent and hollow as a shell. Another woman would have hesitated before entering, but not Mrs. Flynn. She went in like the March wind blowing across the world outside and quickly did what had to be done, sweeping the room, stripping the bed and making it anew, with no thought at all for her late departed roomer.

The wind rattled the window as she finished, rain flailed the glass. *Even the bloody elements are against me,* she thought, for she was a greedy one and her greed couldn't wait.

Now out of the room she swept and down the stairs. There was the sign in the vestibule which had to be hung no matter the weather. Stooping, she snatched it up and opened the outer door to be met with a rush of wind and icy rain that took her breath but didn't stop her. Out she stepped onto the proud-high stoop of the decaying brownstone, hung the sign on its appointed hook and popped back into the vestibule shaking herself like a wet hen. It was done now, the bait set for the proper fish. The trouble was the terrible March weather.

From a front window, peering through a gray curtain, she watched the desolate street, which was now half-obscured by a blinding fall of icy sleet. Finally out of the dim veil a man appeared. Once at the house, he stopped and looked up, caught by the creaking music of the sign swinging wildly in the wind. Moments later up the steps he came and rang the bell. The door swung open in his face and there stood Mrs. Flynn, chin thrust out, sharp eyes probing him.

"I saw your sign," he began.

"I've a room to let," she answered quickly, noting his clothes which were neat enough, but not quality. "Will you look at it?"

"I will, but first . . ."

"It'll be ten a week if you like it, payment in advance."

He grinned at this and said, "I'll take a quick look if you don't mind."

She led him up the stairs, showed him the room, bed, bureau, lamp and closet, making no excuses for the cracked ceiling and ancient wallpaper.

"A good old-fashioned room. Very comfortable," he observed.

"You'll have it?"

"I've already taken it," he said and out came his wallet, well-worn, but of good leather and well-accommodated with bills, one of which he deftly plucked from among the others and handed to her.

"That should keep me for ten weeks," he said, smiling when he saw her eyes light up. "Unless you raise the ante."

"Ten it is and ten it'll be," she answered quickly, not wanting to lose one like this. "I'm Mrs. Flynn, and what did you say your name was? I'll need it for the receipts."

"John Walker, and you can forget the receipts."

"Ah, you're too trusting. I'll slip them under your door, or I wouldn't rest."

"If it'll make you feel better," he said, moving to the door. "I'm going for my bag."

She followed him down the stairs and shivered at the front door. "A terrible day," she observed. "Maybe you'll have a spot of tea before you go out in that?"

"Thanks. Maybe when I get back," he answered and left.

Back to her place at the window she flew to watch him vanish in the swirling veil of snow that was falling now. The mad March day no longer mattered, for this time she had the right one, a roomer with money actually in his possession.

John Walker returned in half an hour, looking like a snowman, and she was waiting, pot, cups, saucers, best silver and linen there in the high-ceilinged parlor. "Put your bag down and come in," she said, taking his arm.

He laughed and allowed himself to be led through the folding door. "Very nice," he remarked of the room as she poured. "Very pleasant."

"A bit old-fashioned, but I like it," she answered, handing him his cup and saucer.

It was good dark tea, steaming and almost black, demanding sugar and cream, which he added and stirred. Then he raised his eyes to see her smiling at him.

"Nothing like a good cup of proper tea on a day like this," she said. "I was afraid it wouldn't fetch you."

"Oh, but it does, especially the way you make it."

"Without no dirty little teabag floating in a bit of tinted water," she laughed, slapping her thigh. "Now mind you, drink that while it's hot."

It was a good beginning, exactly the way she'd wanted it, and now she gave thanks to the madness of the day outside; the snow had stopped and freezing rain slashed at the windows again.

Tea's the grand beverage, thought Mrs. Flynn, recalling Mr. Walker's sudden shyness when she offered to bring a cup to his room now and then. The pleasure was all hers, for the man in him had conceded to comfort. That was part of the plan, to keep him happy as a bird while she went about the business of discovering what she wanted to know.

But Mr. Walker, pleasant and outgoing as he was, didn't reveal himself so easily for all his willingness to talk at length and sit to two and three cups of fine Irish tea. Nor did his room give up any secret about himself, though she fine-combed it daily for the evidence she wanted before acting.

It was his money she was after, and he had it. She was sure of that as of the sun coming up each day, but where was he keeping it? Not in the bank. He wasn't the type. She was convinced of that.

For four weeks she pursued her routine, waiting till he left the house in the morning, then running up the stairs with broom and duster to clean and search, but to no avail. He kept no money in his room.

On the fifth week she gave up searching. At the end of the sixth week she decided to send him packing, when she found the money she was sure he had, neatly tucked in his extra shoes and covered by a pair of dirty socks. Out it came, ten crisp hundred-dollar bills which she counted twice with trembling hands.

"Ah! I knew it," she moaned and counted the money again for the pleasure of counting. Then went below for a cup of tea and to make preparations. It was April now, a fine day with the warm, fresh fever of spring in the air, which was not to her liking. But at times April is as daft as March and by afternoon the air grew raw and the balmy air freshened till by dark it was battering the city in wild gusts.

Mrs. Flynn waited at the window, but Mr. Walker didn't show at his regular time. It was ten when he finally plodded up the high stoop and opened the door.

"Ah, it's Mr. Walker, and late and chilly you are," she greeted him with in the hall. "Your tea's waiting and steaming."

But for once he refused. He was tired, he said, a bad day, and went up the stairs to his room.

The first time he refused her tea. It was a bad sign. Later, she heard him descend the stairs and out he went. The door closed with a dismal sound and opened again ten seconds later.

She flew to the folding door and pushed it aside. "Something wrong, Mr. Walker?"

"Nothing at all," he said, starting to mount the stairs and halting with a frown on his face.

"What is it, Mr. Walker?"

"I'm leaving tomorrow," he said. "For Chicago."

"You're joking," she said, turning pale.

"I wish I were, but I'm not. Well, it was a pleasant stay."

"Ah, then, a last cup of tea," she said desperately.

"Thanks, but it'll keep me awake. I've got to be up for an early start," he replied, starting up the stairs again.

"For old times sake," she called after him. "And it won't keep you awake. You'll sleep like a baby."

He paused again, smiled and said, "Well, then," and came down the stairs.

She poured for him in the high-ceilinged parlor and they chatted a while. Then he went above, with the tea she'd poisoned already doing its work.

By morning he was dead. "A fine man," she said as they carried him down the high stoop under a gray blanket. Then she handed the policeman his coat, bag and a pack of cigarettes. "Not much," she said. "But, then, he doesn't need much where he's going."

"That's right," the policeman answered and out of the hall he went. The stretcher was already in the wagon. The policeman descended the stoop, handed over coat and bag and watched the morgue wagon move off, then walked away.

Mrs. Flynn closed the door and flew up the stairs to her late tenant's room. Panting, she entered it and went to the closet. There were the shoes she hadn't given up, with the dirty socks still stuffed in them. Greedily, she snatched them up and pulled out the socks, but the money was gone.

Took it with him, he did. Why didn't I look through his pockets before I called the police? she groaned and went below, sick with her terrible mistake, but not too sick for a cup of tea.

She poured for herself, sat for a while in the high-ceilinged parlor, then got up and went out on the stoop to hang her deadly sign once more—ROOM TO LET.

DOUBLE TROUBLE

by Robert Edmond Alter

Mr. Darby lowered the .22 pistol and looked at the dresser clock. 7:17. Thirteen minutes before his regular awaking time. That thirteen minutes must now be used to take care of the few details that were not a part of his usual morning schedule. A few details, yes, but mighty important to his future security. He chuckled and allowed himself ten seconds to contemplate his handiwork with a judicious yet proud eye.

A .22 pistol is not noted for its noise, and when one fires a .22 through a bulky pillow the ensuing explosion is but a minor *pop!* And such a tidy little hole it makes, too. No mess. Mr. Darby was glad of that. He had a very orderly mind.

He set the pistol aside and went around his wife's bed, squatted down and lifted the blanket, folding it up on the bed just so. Then he unzipped the side of the mattress cover. His wife had never had much of an imagination . . . no more than any old maid who hides her money in her mattress. Mr. Darby had been married to Mrs. Darby for two years; and for one year he'd known exactly where she hid her money. Getting to the money had been the problem.

His wife had claimed to be an invalid—completely bed-ridden (a claim which Mr. Darby secretly doubted, but could not disprove as he was away at the office each day from 8:30 to 6:30; but he'd always suspected that his wife slipped out of bed after he left the house, and pottered around until his return). She'd led him a dog's life . . . always nagging, always complaining; forever making him wait on her hand and foot; up the stairs, down the stairs; fetch this, take away that. . . . And all the time he'd known that she was lolling her fat body on top of her money, and he hadn't been able to get to it. Not until this morning. Now she didn't have a word to say . . . not a word, and her silence was like tender music to his ears.

He reached inside the mattress and began drawing out plump packets of money, packets of fives, tens, twenties, fifties. . . . There was no time to count it, no need, really. He knew she was rich, knew she didn't keep her money in a bank, and would have nothing to do with stocks and bonds. He'd known these facts *before* he married her. One does not marry a fat, disgusting, crabby old woman of fifty for love.

He fetched a briefcase from his closet and stacked the money neatly inside. Then—it was just 7:30—he went into the bathroom. He returned to the quiet bedroom with his toothbrush and razor, placed these articles in the briefcase and followed them with shorts and socks. That was all the traveling equipment he could safely afford to take. If he tried to leave the house with a suitcase his nosy neighbors would wonder, and he couldn't have that. It didn't matter; he would buy new clothes in Paris.

Dressed, he went to the door carrying the briefcase, but paused to look back at his wife's bed with a smile. "Have a nice rest, dear," he said solicitously.

Coming down the stairs Mr. Darby glanced at the hall clock—7:40—and nodded, as though confirming his unbreakable rule for punctuality. From now until he left the bus downtown at 8:50, everything must follow the exact time pattern he'd adhered to each morning for the past two years. It wasn't for nothing that his neighbors said of him: "You can set your clock by Darby." And this morning, this very special morning, nothing must appear amiss; every minute must be accounted for, every second must be in its proper position in the Darby time schedule.

The kitchen clock said 7:43 as Mr. Darby placed three limp strips of bacon on the pre-heated grill. But he checked himself, staring with a look of witlessness at what he'd done. He only ate *two* pieces of bacon in the morning . . . habit had placed the third strip for his wife. He giggled weakly, and shook his head, shocked by the slip. "I must watch that," he warned himself.

He made a very elaborate gesture in selecting *his* two eggs from the refrigerator.

His eggs frying, his toast toasting, he had his half-glass of prune juice and looked at the clock again. 7:48. Time to fetch the morning paper and let Tabby in. He trotted down the hall, smiling to himself.

Letting Tabby in each morning always gave him a perverse pleasure. Mrs. Darby had been like Craig's wife—very meticulous about her home and furnishings, and she'd had no use at all for Tabby the cat, complaining that "the filthy little beast" shed fur balls. So every morning, without a word said to his wife, Mr. Darby would let Tabby inside the house. A minor rebellion against his wife's tyranny, one that had given him many a secret chuckle.

Mr. Darby went out on the front porch, picked up the rolled newspaper, and called softly, "Tabby-tabby-tabby."

His next-door neighbor, the widow Reese, looked up from her weeding and smiled at him, but glanced at her wristwatch before she spoke. "Why, Mr. Darby," she called. "Either you're two minutes early this morning, or I'm two minutes slow."

As a rule Mr. Darby felt offended by Mrs. Reese's chiding remarks concerning his punctuality; but this morning he welcomed the observation. Still—it was vexing to think that something might have gone wrong with his clocks and that he *was* two minutes ahead of his schedule. A little thing like that might call unwanted attention to him. But no . . . it was more likely that Mrs. Reese's watch was slow, and he said as much.

"I'm afraid it must be your watch, Mrs. Reese. I check my clocks at night with the telephone operator . . . they're electric, you know."

Mrs. Reese nodded. "If I know you, Mr. Darby, you're right. Correct time is one thing we can *always* count on you for."

Tabby, sleek and low to the ground, scooted from a hedge and made a beeline through the front doors. Mrs. Reese, following the hurried movement, smiled again. "Tabby is certainly *your* pet, Mr. Darby," she said, and something about her smile and the look in her eyes seemed to suggest to Mr. Darby that she understood his ordeal.

Mr. Darby glanced at his own wristwatch—7:51—and said, "Excuse me now, Mrs. Reese . . . my eggs are just about done."

He hurried back to the kitchen, saved his eggs from a crisp fate, gave the mewing cat her saucer of milk, and took his breakfast into the dining room. The dining-room clock said it was 7:55 precisely as Mr. Darby tucked his napkin into his collar.

He had finished his breakfast—8:10—and had just started to unroll his morning paper when the hall phone rang. Frowning, Mr. Darby left the table and went into the hall.

"Hello, Darb?" the voice said in his ear. "Didn't wake you up, did I?" Then the voice laughed and said something to someone else that Mr. Darby couldn't catch.

He wasn't really surprised by the call; in fact, he'd been half-expecting it. Smitty, an office clerk, always got such a boot out of ribbing him about his punctuality.

"No, no, Smitty," Mr. Darby said. "I was just having breakfast."

The voice laughed again. "That's just what I told the gang, Darb. I said: 'Even on his vacation old Darb will be sticking to that time schedule like glue.' And was I right?"

Mr. Darby forced an unnecessary smile. "Yes, that's right. I'm always on schedule."

"Well, Darb, have a nice two weeks, hear? Plenty of time for you to do all the housework, eh? Lots of dusting and polishing and cleaning, eh, Darb? Ho-ho! See you in a couple of weeks, boy!"

Mr. Darby put the phone down and looked around at the quiet house.

"That's what you think," he murmured. "I've cleaned this place for the last time."

He started back to his newspaper feeling very pleased with himself. His neighbors had no idea that his vacation commenced that morning. When he left the house at 8:30 they'd think he was off to work as usual. Not one of them would have the least concern for him until they noticed he hadn't returned home at 6:30. By 7:30 they might even begin to wonder about him; and by 8:30 they'd probably begin to worry over his sudden pattern break. And possibly by 9:30 they would even come to his house to inquire—maybe phone the police.

It didn't matter. When he left the bus downtown he was going to take a taxi to the airport, and there catch the 9:20 flight to New York. From the International Airport he would take the 10:30 flight to Paris. At the earliest possible time that the police could discover his wife . . . he would be setting down in Europe. After that—the selection of a new name, the purchase of a false passport, and . . . the vanishing point!

When the doorbell rang it was as though someone had slipped up behind him and shouted BOO! in his ear. Mr. Darby dropped his paper and looked at the clock with a sort of wild fear. 8:21. What fool would be ringing his doorbell at this time of morning? Why?

He pushed back his chair and hurried to the front door.

A smiling man greeted him on his own porch. The man held an open box in one hand that was neatly packed with an array of brushes and weird-looking tools; in the other hand a heavy bag with the trade name stamped in gold letters.

"Mr. Darby? I have your order here, sir."

Mr. Darby blinked. "My order?"

"Yes, your brushes . . . or rather your wife's. Heh-heh."

Mr. Darby felt very dense. "My wife's?"

The brushman's smile turned hesitant. "Yes, sir. The brushes your wife ordered from me last week."

Mr. Darby looked at his watch. 8:22.

"I don't understand," he said absently. "How could she order any brushes? She's an invalid, bedridden."

The brushman's smile was now a doubtful-looking thing. He glanced at the house numerals on the mailbox as though checking his bearings, then pulled a paper from his coat-pocket.

"But you *are* Mr. Darby, aren't you? I have her order here: one sink brush—nylon; one hairbrush—nylon; one hand lotion—Blue Memory; one deodorant—Pine Scent. . . . It's all for a Mrs. Elmo Darby. She met me right here at the door last week . . . uh-Monday, I think."

So it was true! The thing he'd suspected all along. His wife had not been an invalid. Mr. Darby raged inwardly. Two years of tyranny; waiting on her like a slave, housecleaning on Sundays, cooking her meals, fetching and carrying, ever up-the-stairs-down-the-stairs. . . . He was almost sorry now that he hadn't awakened her just before he had. . . .

8:23.

"Yes, yes," Mr. Darby snapped, and made to close the door. "We don't want it."

The brushman gawked at him. "Not want it, sir? But your wife ordered the things, Mr. Darby. Perhaps if I might see Mrs. Darby for a moment . . ."

Mr. Darby started. "Do what? No! *Oh no!* You can't see her . . . she's asleep . . . uh—eating her breakfast . . . she's still in bed." He glanced at his watch again. His behavior was too erratic, he knew. The brushman would begin to think something was wrong with him. Pattern-pattern-pattern. Nothing must look amiss. There was still time to take care of this man calmly and then get on with the schedule.

"How much is the bill?" Mr. Darby asked.

The brushman's smile was on firm ground again. He looked at the bill. "Well, let's see here, Mr. Darby . . . it all totals to four-twenty-one. That's the tax too, you understand. That's . . ."

"Yes, yes." 8:24. Mr. Darby reached for his wallet . . . but stalled, remembering where all his money was. "Just a moment, please," he mumbled. He hurried back into the dining room and opened the briefcase, his fingers fumbling and snatching for a packet of money.

The brushman's mouth dropped a bit when he looked at the bill Mr. Darby had handed him. "A fifty-dollar bill? I don't know that I can make change for . . ."

Mr. Darby almost let his groan be heard. He'd thought it was a five. He snatched the fifty back, saying, "Just a moment. I have more—I mean, I have smaller."

8:26 the dining-room clock informed him as he fumbled through the packets of money again. "I must get ahold of myself," he hissed desperately. "The man will think I'm balmy." He almost ran back to the front door.

How could one man be as slow as the brushman was counting out the change? Mr. Darby wanted to strangle him.

"Four-twenty-one out of five, yes, sir. And fifty cents makes four-seventy-one, and a quarter makes four-ninety-six, and let's see . . . one penny, two pennies, three pennies . . . that's four-ninety-nine . . . let's see, must have another penny here somewhere in all this . . ."

Mr. Darby put his empty hand to his face to rub his features out of whack. 8:28. "It's all right," he said. "Forget the penny."

"No, no. Have it right here, sir. There you are—*oops!* Almost dropped it. There; that makes five, and thank you, Mr. Darby."

"Yes, yes, that's all right. 'Bye." Mr. Darby closed the door.

Immediately the brushman knocked on it.

Mr. Darby slapped his forehead, then collected himself and opened the door again. The brushman was smiling at him hesitantly, holding out a fat package. "You forgot to take your order, Mr. Darby."

Finally the door was closed. Mr. Darby was inside with the package of brushes that would never be used, and the brushman was gone.

8:30.

Mr. Darby snatched up his briefcase, snatched his hat, cleared his throat, adjusted his tie, and opened the front door. He stepped onto the porch, closing the door behind him for the last time.

Everything was all right now. He was still right on schedule . . . a little excited, but he'd walk that off. He started down the driveway, clipping along at his usual "time's-passing-don't-waste-it" stride.

Mrs. Reese looked up smiling. "My watch will be correct now, Mr. Darby. 8:30 sharp. I can always set it by you."

Mr. Darby smiled, walking on.

"Did your dear wife enjoy her breakfast this morning, Mr. Darby?" she called after him. "How's her pain?"

Mr. Darby's sense of humor cost him four seconds. He paused and looked back. "I gave her a very special breakfast this morning," he said. "She's feeling no pain at all."

The clock in the administration building of the airport said 10:15 as the passengers for the Paris flight started filing through the gate. Mr. Darby was feeling very good, very good indeed. He felt as though he had all the time in the world. All his problems, his fears, seemed trivial now. He felt so good he didn't even look twice at the man in overcoat and snapbrim who was checking the passengers' papers.

But when Mr. Darby held out his ticket and stamped passport, the man in the overcoat and snapbrim held out his wallet—showing Mr. Darby a shiny metal badge.

"You'll have to come with me, Mr. Darby. I'm arresting you on suspicion of murder." Perhaps he said more than that, but if he did Mr. Darby missed it. His brain was a whirligig running wild.

"How—how—" he sounded like an Indian greeting strangers as the detective led him off, "—how could you've found out so soon?"

The detective couldn't seem to keep his smile down. "You

and your wife were certainly methodical people, Mr. Darby. Never a moment's variance in your daily schedules."

"In *our* schedules? What schedule did my wife have?"

"Didn't you know?" The detective seemed more amused than ever. "Well, at 7:49 each morning you'd bring in the paper and cat. Could set your watch by it, Mrs. Reese, your neighbor said. Then at 8:30 you'd leave the house for work. And at 8:40 your wife would open the front door and throw the cat outside."

"But this morning Mrs. Darby *didn't* throw the cat out; so Mrs. Reese became worried—knowing your wife was a sick woman—and went over to your house to investigate; and so . . ."

HEIST IN PIANISSIMO

by Talmage Powell

Judy put her hands over her ears. "I won't hear another word of it, Davie! We're not criminals, you know."

In the moonlight beside the lake, she was a lovely, petite brunette. I took quick steps after her as she flounced her skirt and moved toward my jalopy, which was parked nearby.

"Okay, okay," I said. "Just pretend I never opened my big mouth."

I held the door for her to get in the car.

"The very idea, Davie, the two of us robbing the bank! Why, we come from decent, respectable backgrounds. We've never had a mark against us, even when we were in our teens. We're about the last pair of young people anybody in town would associate with a bank robbery."

I went around the car and got in. "I know," I said. "So forget it, will you?"

"Give me a cigarette."

I handed her the package. She sneaked a look at me. Then she smoked in silence as I started the car, turned it around, and headed back toward town.

"Davie . . ." she said in the murmuring tone that indicated a mountain of thought behind a single word. Davie anticipated it.

"Uh-huh?"

"Whatever gave you the thought?"

"Oh, I don't know. Just wishing you and I could make with life while we're still young, I guess. Maybe it was looking at old man Peterson, your boss at the bank, or Mr. Harper at the hardware store. Tomorrow morning, for example, they'll be standing not six inches from the spot where they started standing thirty or forty years ago."

"Both our bosses are nice people, Davie. They've bought homes, raised families . . ."

". . . and seen the same faces, talked the same talk, moved

through the same routine day after day. They might as well be vegetables, Judy. One day or a million days adds up to the same for them. Because they've never lived. They've just existed in a kind of vacuum. Now it's too late for them. A few more years of the same malarkey and they'll be planted out in marble orchard and somebody else will have moved into their same dull spots."

"It's best not to think about those things, Davie."

"Sometimes you can't help it," I said. "Not if there is somebody special that you want special things for."

She reached forward and turned on the car radio loud enough to drown out my voice. But we'd ridden less than half a mile when she turned it down again.

"Now mind you, Davie," she murmured, "I'm not planning on doing anything so crazy, but wouldn't it be wonderful if we woke up tomorrow morning or the next day and had fifty or sixty thousand dollars?"

"That's what I tried to point out, there at the lake," I said. "It isn't like we were turning into pathological criminals. We just do this one thing. We keep right on about our business until the furor over the robbery dies down. Then I tell Mr. Harper one day that I've got an offer of a job in California. We get married. Our friends give us a going-away party. We promise to write, but somehow we never do. You know how those things go.

"A few years from now, we won't even remember what this grubby mill town looks like. Instead, we'll have bought a business of our own, worked hard, and retired by the time we're thirty-five. Then we swim in Miami Beach, or play golf in Pasadena.

"I sure don't intend to squander the money, Judy. Just a break, the opportunity to get started, to make it for ourselves while we're young, that's all I was thinking about. It's no worse than the old financial barons who conspired to take oil lands from the Indians, or who entered political deals to use public domain for railroad right of way."

Nervously, Judy lit a second cigarette from her first.

I peeped at her without turning my head, and sighed. " 'Course, I guess it was wishful thinking, like we all do at times, and I'm sorry I brought it up."

"It would be nice," Judy said. "Yes, it really would."

"If we had a kid or two, we could give them a decent chance, too."

We rolled through the edges of town, toward Judy's house. Suddenly, she reached and touched my hand. "Don't make the turn, Davie. I don't feel like going in. Let's go to the Jiffy-burger and have a sandwich and a malt."

"Okay," I said.

At the drive-in, I found a spot not too close to other cars. We munched on hamburgers without saying anything for a while.

Then Judy stirred in her seat as if her muscles were cramped. "Davie . . ."

"Uh-huh?"

"It's true that about seventy-five thousand dollars will be in my cage Friday, because of the Landers Mills payday and all their payroll checks."

"I know," I said, "it's one thing that got me thinking."

"Well, I'm certainly not taken with your thieving ideas, Dave Hartshell! But . . . just making believe . . . how would you get the money out of the bank without the guard arresting you before you reached the front door?"

I slouched in the seat and took a big pull at my malt straw. "Oh, I'd pull the heist in pianissimo."

"In what?"

"Pianissimo, Judy. That's a music term. It means very softly. I'd take the money so softly the guard would smile as he held the door for me to leave the bank."

She pulled upright, leaned over to have a closer look at me.

"Davie, how would you go about keeping a bank robbery pian-whatever-it-is?"

"I'd prepare the Friday morning deposit from the store a little earlier than usual," I said. "I'd bring it over to the bank just like always, in the leather and canvas money satchel.

"I'd pass the deposit over to you, Judy, like any other morning. Only when you got all through, I'd stroll out of the bank with the satchel crammed with the biggest denomination bills in your cage."

She jerked erect, bumping her head on the top of my jalopy. "Of all the nerve, Davie! Asking me to risk my reputation, everything . . ."

"You wouldn't risk a thing, honey," I said. "All the tune's in harmony, like in pianissimo. We fix up a note in advance, printed with crayon on a sheet of dime-store paper, which we're careful not to get any fingerprints on. Except yours. You'll have to handle it."

"Davie, I do believe you've taken to secret drinking!"

"Just an occasional beer," I said. "This note, which you'll carry into the bank with you Friday morning, says, 'Hand over the money or I'll kill you on the spot.'

"After I'm out of the bank a half hour or so and the place starts getting crowded, you let the note flutter to the floor. Then you keel over in a real bad faint."

She was to the point now where she stared at me like she was helpless to move her eyes.

"I faint," she said finally.

"And right at first when you come around," I said, "you're kind of vague. Then it begins to come back to you. You get excited, and scared, and darn near hysterical. Since I'm young, slender, and dark, you ask them if they caught the middle-age, medium-built, ruddy man. Then they have found the note on the floor of your cage, and they say, 'Which man?' And you say, 'He slipped his coat open to show me a gun he was carrying. I put the money in a sack he handed to me. He slipped it under his coat. I tried to raise the alarm, but a terrible, empty blackness was rolling over me.' "

"A terrible, empty blackness," Judy said.

"You're the one girl I know who can really cool it, Judy. Then you leave it lay at that point. Not too complicated. Not too much description."

"There's just one thing wrong with it, Davie. You remember the bank robbery a few months ago over in Conover?"

"Sure. That's what gave me the idea of . . ."

"The teller had to take a lie-detector test, Davie. It's routine. They've anticipated the kind of thing you're planning."

"And I have anticipated *them*, doll," I said, feeling pretty good at the moment.

"Have you really?" Her voice was cool, and just a little pitying.

I didn't let the womanish attitude nettle me. Merely patted her small, sweet hand. "That's where Mr. Eggleston comes in," I said.

"Eggleston?"

"An old gentleman I met in the Wee Barrel."

"Davie! I've practically *begged* you to stay out of that tavern on your way home from work!"

"This Eggleston is quite a guy," I said, warming to the

subject. "Neat, unobtrusive man, with impeccable clothes. Never see him with a gray hair out of place."

"Well, I don't care to know any of the hangers-on in the Wee Barrel." Judy stuck her nose in the air. After a few seconds, it lowered slightly. "When did you fit him into your plan?"

"After I found out he'd once been a metaphysical therapist in Los Angeles."

"Sounds like he was a quack."

"But definitely, Judy. They finally ran him out of town. He's also rigged stock deals, sold salted mines, and headed up drives to raise funds for nonexistent charities."

"You seem to know him quite well, Davie," she said, a note of warning in her voice.

"Yeah, we got to be pretty close friends after he found out my girl friend worked in the bank."

"I guess you'll have to get the rest of it out of your system before you start the car, Davie. And it's too far for me to walk home."

"This Eggleston," I said, "when he was in the business of treating nervous and emotionally troubled people, he used a lot of hypnotism. He's really great with it, Judy. You should see some of the stunts he pulls in the Wee Barrel. One night he gave Shorty Connors the post-hypnotic suggestion to stand on his head. And darned if Shorty didn't try to upend himself five minutes after he came out of the trance just like Eggleston had told him."

"I begin to see the light," Judy said thinly.

"Sure, hon. That silly lie-detector machine won't mean a thing. You'll face it under the influence of post-hypnotic suggestion. The cops will hunt a nonexistent robber and never suspect that . . ."

"I," she said, "am not the slightest bit interested."

She called me at seven-thirty the next morning, a half-hour earlier than usual.

At five-thirty that afternoon, we entered Mr. Eggleston's hotel room together.

Mr. Eggleston made a small bow when I introduced him. "David, she is every bit as lovely as you stated. It is indeed a pleasure to know you, my dear Judy. May I call room service and get you anything? Perhaps an aperitif?"

"No, thanks."

"No need to be nervous, my dear. The process is painless. You will, in fact, feel more relaxed than you have in quite awhile."

"Let's just get it over with," Judy said, worrying her small handbag in her hands.

"Quite."

Mr. Eggleston crossed the room, partially closed the blinds, and motioned toward a big easychair.

Judy sat down like she was forcing her knees to bend. Mr. Eggleston stood smiling and quiet before her.

"To be wholly successful, my dear, I must have your total cooperation. Put yourself in my hands completely."

Judy gulped slightly. I thought she was going to back out. But she must have thought of all the money that would be in her teller's cage tomorrow.

Mr. Eggleston's manner was gentle and comforting. He drew a light occasional chair close to her and sat down. From his pocket, he took a shiny piece of metal about the size of a quarter.

"Focus your eyes on the coin, Judy, and blank your mind. . . . Relax completely. . . . Offer no resistance. . . . It is so pleasant to relax. . . ."

He continued to talk soothingly. Judy's lids began to droop.

"You are sleepy, my dear . . . so gently and delightfully sleepy. . . . Sleep. . . . You are going to sleep. . . . How pleasant to sleep. . . . You are asleep, Judy . . . deeply asleep . . . very deeply, Judy."

Mr. Eggleston began to draw away from her slowly. "You are in a deep, deep trance, Judy. You will remain in this trance until I count to three and snap my fingers."

My throat was starting to get a little dry. I evenly shifted from one foot to the other.

Mr. Eggleston glanced at me. "She's a most interesting subject, David. A very wonderful subject. Proof of her intelligence. The moron cannot be hypnotized, you know."

He returned his attention to Judy. "When at last I count to three and snap my fingers, Judy, you will awaken from the trance immediately. Your conscious mind will remember nothing. To your conscious mind it will seem as if you have merely drifted off for a few seconds. But your subconscious will retain everything that is done during the trance to prepare you psychologically and physiologically for what is ahead. Is all this clear?"

"Yes, it is." Judy's voice was so everydayish and normal that I wondered for a second if she was faking the trance. But I knew better. There'd be no point in it. And I remembered how natural Shorty Connors had sounded while Mr. Eggleston had him under.

"Now, Judy," Mr. Eggleston said, "there are a few things we must understand and make clear at the outset. There is nothing magical or supernatural in what we are doing. I can merely assist you. I cannot force you to do anything which you are absolutely determined not to do. For example, I could not force you to remove your clothing in the public square unless you had, in the secret depths of your personality, an exhibitionist urge to do such a thing. Do you understand?"

"Yes."

"If you could stretch a moral point and obtain a great deal of money without injuring anyone, would you do so?"

"Why not?"

"Would you tell a straight-out lie for ten dollars?"

"No."

"A hundred dollars?"

Judy didn't hesitate. "No."

"A thousand dollars?"

Judy hesitated.

"Fifty thousand dollars?" Mr. Eggleston persisted.

Judy rushed the answer: "Any day in the week! Just any old day!"

Mr. Eggleston glanced at me with a satisfied smile, which I returned rather weakly while wiping beads of perspiration from my face.

Then Mr. Eggleston returned to his subject: "Judy, since you are a bright and intelligent girl, I'm sure you know the basic principle of the lie detector. When a person tells a lie, he or she experiences a slight rise in pulse rate, heartbeat, blood pressure. The graph registers these changes and the operator of the machine determines if a person has told the truth."

"I understand," Judy said.

"Good. The reason for these physiological changes lies in the psyche, the subconscious. Mind over matter, so to speak."

"I understand," Judy repeated.

"But that is a two-way street, my dear. Isn't it? If the

subconscious can control the pulse rate, the subconscious can also ignore it. Tomorrow you will tell a lie in police headquarters. Your conscious mind will recognize it as a lie. But to your subconscious, in that instant, it will not matter. That is the whole crux of the thing, Judy. It's simple. Very simple. Your subconscious will not care one whit whether or not you have told a lie on that single subject." Mr. Eggleston's voice became a soft, but insistent lash. "Your subconscious will experience a momentary moral lapse when you describe the man who robbed the bank. Hence, you will exhibit none of the physiological symptoms for the graph to record. Repeat after me, Judy: It will not matter whether I am lying about the description of the bank robber."

"It—will—not—matter—"

"You must accept this thought in such a way as to be comfortable, Judy. Are you comfortable?"

"Yes."

"Good. Now we shall awaken. One . . . two . . . three . . ."

I started slightly when his fingers snapped.

Judy opened her eyes, gazed at me blankly a moment, then looked at Mr. Eggleston.

He was paying her no attention. "David, tomorrow night at ten, I shall call at your rooming house for the five thousand dollars you've agreed to pay me."

Judy said, "I must have dozed off a second. When do we begin with this hypnotism?"

"We have finished with it," Eggleston smiled.

She frowned. "Is that true, Davie?"

I nodded.

"But I don't feel any different," Judy said. "Are you sure?"

"Positively," Mr. Eggleston said. He patted me on the shoulder. "And it's a brilliant idea, my boy, one I might have come up with myself!"

I woke the next morning, Friday, with about two hours total sleep during the preceding night. My stomach was jerky, and I nicked myself while shaving. I had a cup of coffee for an indigestible breakfast.

I walked around the block twice, waiting for the hardware store to open. Inside, I had the bank deposit prepared in record-breaking time. I had to kill several minutes arrangeing a display of fishing gear for the simple reason that I didn't think it wise to be the very first customer in the bank.

Feeling as if every eye in the grubby factory town was focused on me, I forced myself past the glass and brass doors of the bank. The guard, Mr. Sevier, was looking directly at me.

Normally, Mr. Sevier appears to me as a kindly middle-aged man with an elfin sort of face and tufts of white hair in his ears. Today, he grew horns; his skin was a threatening purple; there was brimstone in his slitted eyes.

"Good morning, Mr. Sevier."

"Nice to see you, Davie." He slapped me on the back as I passed.

Behind her teller's wicket, Judy gave me a warm smile. She appeared to have slept quite well, and I wondered if maybe I shouldn't have let Mr. Eggleston put me under also.

I handed the heavy leather and canvas bag to Judy. She opened it, checked the deposit.

Nobody paid any attention to my lingering at Judy's window. There was just enough early business to keep the other employees occupied. Anyhow, everyone in the bank knew that Judy and I were collecting pennies in a joint account toward the day we could be married.

With a nod that no one else noticed, she finally returned the satchel to me.

My heart started going like sixty. I felt as if the weight of the bag were pulling me to one side, making me walk out of the bank at a crazy angle.

I was almost at the doors when Judy called my name quietly.

I had to stop right beside Mr. Sevier.

"Don't forget lunch, Davie," Judy said.

"I won't."

She blew me a little kiss. Mr. Sevier chuckled fondly as he gave me a little punch on the shoulder.

I went to the parking lot half a block away and collapsed in my car.

I tugged my collar with my finger, got a lungful of air, started the car, and drove casually to the hardware store. By the time I parked behind the store, I'd transferred the money to the heavy brown paper bag and stuffed it under the seat of the car. I was practically twitching with nervous eagerness to count the money. Driving along with commonplace innocence, the important work taking place with my free hand below window level, I'd caught only glances of the neatly banded money. But I knew there was plenty. I'd never seen so many stacks of fifties and hundreds in one place in all my life—except in the bank. I was certainly grateful to Landers Mills for paying but twice a month, on the first and fifteenth.

I started to lock the car, then decided against it. So far, everything was perfect. I'd driven directly from the bank, in plain view of the town. Judy and I were experiencing a routine, commonplace day. I wasn't in the habit of locking the jalopy this time of year. The money was safely out of sight. I went into the store.

Fortunately, there were customers to help pass the morning. Even so, I had to make three trips to the gent's room inside of an hour.

Then at ten fifty-six by the clock on the far wall, which had a pendulum behind a fly-specked front that advertised Maney's Merrygrow Manure, the waiting was all over.

Like a well-fed, full-bosomed turkey with a gray topknot, Mrs. Threckle came to the door of the office, spoke my name, and motioned to me frantically.

I hurried to her. "What is it, Mrs. Threckle?"

"Terrible thing . . ." she gasped, "terrible . . . a bank robbery . . . They've got Judy at police headquarters. . . ."

I had to grab the office door framing to keep from folding to the floor like a collapsing letter Z. This part wasn't an act, either. I thought wildly: They've caught her, and she's trying to protect me, going it alone. . . .

"Your poor, dear boy!" Mrs. Threckle said. "You must get down there right away. I'll explain to Mr. Harper."

I could think of several other directions more preferable. Then Mrs. Threckle saved me from a nervous breakdown.

"She hasn't been hurt, Davie. There was no shooting. They've merely taken her down to get a description of the robber."

Several minutes later, a jalopy full of holdup money was parked in plain view in front of police headquarters. Inside the building there was turmoil. Each time I tried to stop a hurrying policeman, he would jerk his thumb over his shoulder, pointing deeper into the building. "Busy, bud."

Finally I spotted old Silas Garth ambling placidly from a doorway. Silas has been on the force just about as long as the town has had a charter. He paused in the corridor, more intent on picking something from his teeth than picking up a bank robber.

"Mr. Garth . . ."

"Oh, hello there, Davie. Guess you're looking for Judy."

"Yes, sir. Is she . . ."

"Simmer down, son. She's fine. Come on back in the squad room and we'll have a game of checks until Hoskins and Crowley and that lie-detector technician are through with her."

Poor Judy, I thought. Going through hell, that's what.

"What happened, Mr. Garth?"

He shrugged as we walked down the corridor together. "Yegg came walking in, let Judy have a peep at a gun, gave her a second to read the note he shoved in her hand, and walked back out with about sixty-five thousand dollars in a brown paper bag."

"Yowie!" I yelped. "Sixty-five thou—Is there that much money in the world?"

"Shore is, Davie. And I'm feared this hoodlum made it out of town."

"How come you say that, Mr. Garth?"

"Judy—bless her darling heart—was so paralyzed with fright she couldn't give the alarm right away. And when she realized she was in no danger of the gun, she fainted dead away."

"But you said she was fine!"

He laid his hand on my arm. "She is now, Davie. Take it easy, will you?"

"Was she able to give them a description of the robber?"

"General is all. Middle-aged, ruddy, medium height, sort of heavy-set. My opinion is, he's an old pro at the robbery game, Davie."

"How come you say that, Mr. Garth?"

The old man started putting checkers in their proper squares on a board that rested on a rickety card table. "We got ways of lifting prints nowadays from surfaces like paper. The note he handed Judy had no prints on it but hers. Reckon he knew his prints would identify him." Mr. Garth shook his head. "Be frank with you, Davie, lots of these yeggs get away with it, at least for one or two outings."

"You don't think they'll catch him?"

"I wouldn't make book on it, son. His chances decrease

all the time, of course. Next time out, he may get caught and we'll break our case then."

"Mr. Garth, if you don't mind, I couldn't keep my mind on a checker game right now."

"Sure, Davie." He flung his arm about my shoulders. "We'll go upstairs, son, and see if we can't make it easier on that poor girl."

We went upstairs, and I sought a gent's room while Mr. Garth disappeared into an office. I was pacing the corridor when he opened the office door and came out behind Judy.

She ran straight to me, and I folded her in my arms.

Mr. Garth clucked affectionately. "Judy didn't stretch none of the details of the description, according to the polygraph, Davie. Now you take that girl down the street and buy her a cup of coffee."

I said, "Yes, sir, Mr. Garth!"

Judy and I were still slightly delirious when Mr. Eggleston knocked on my door at ten o'clock that night.

He slipped in quickly, and I closed the door. He looked from me to Judy, a smile dividing his lean, hawkish face.

"Well, kids, we pulled it off!"

"We sure did, Mr. Eggleston, and your five thousand dollars is ready for you."

His eyes went frigid. He pulled a short-nosed gun from his side coat pocket.

"Wh-what is this, Mr. Eggleston?" It was the real thing.

"I've waited all my life for the really big one," he said. "Do you think I'd let a couple of hick kids stand in my way? Now get the money!"

"But Mr. Eggleston . . ."

"All of it! Now! If it hasn't occurred to you, none of us can squeal without implicating himself."

I was unable to move or think for a second. "But if you shoot that gun, Mr. Eggleston, somebody will hear it."

"And you'll be dead. I'm offering you a deal, Davie. Two lives for the money."

"You're crazy," I said.

"No—and don't let the money destroy your sanity, kid. If I shoot the gun, I'll have a good chance of getting away. You won't have any chances, period. I'm willing to make the gamble, Davie. I'm too old, I've waited too long to let this final chance slip away from me."

His cheekbones began to turn white, and he added: "I'll give you ten seconds to make up your mind, David."

I didn't know Judy had risen. Now I felt her pressing against me. She shivered. "Davie . . . he *is* a little mad. He means it!"

"Sure I do," Eggleston said cold-bloodedly. "Six . . . five . . . four . . . three . . ."

"Give him the money, Davie," Judy sobbed, holding onto me wildly.

"In the closet," I said numbly. "The small valise."

Everything around me had a kind of swimming quality. Mr. Eggleston floated to the closet, the valise floated to his hand. He flipped the catch, peeked quickly inside, pressed it closed with his left hand. The gun still on us in his right hand, he floated out the door.

Judy didn't have to work the next day, it being Saturday. I called the store and reported I was too sick to work.

But I was there bright and early Monday morning. There's no better way to impress an employer than being prompt, when you finally decide you're going to be stuck in a job for a mighty long time.

WISH YOU WERE HERE

by Richard Hardwick

The idiosyncrasies of most people end with death and are only rarely recalled afterward, with decreasing frequency and accuracy, in reminiscences of their friends and acquaintances. Martha Adamson, however, true to her form in life, was not like most people in death. Or so it seemed. She was still a bit on the peculiar side.

Charlie Adamson came to me scarcely a month after his wife's funeral. He was pale, and though the afternoon was cool after the rains we had been having almost daily, a fine beading of perspiration stood out on his forehead.

"Buzzy," he said, plopping down in one of the rockers on my porch. My real name is Henry Busby, but as far back as I can remember folks have just called me "Buzzy." "Buzzy," said Charlie, "you knew Martha as well as anybody, including myself. Would you say she might have had any . . . any odd powers?"

"Depends on what you mean by odd, Charlie," I said as diplomatically as possible. I hauled out the old briar and dug it down into the tobacco pouch.

"Well," Charlie went on, "let me ask you something else. Do you believe there's a life after death?"

"I suppose I do. What are you getting at?"

He reached quickly into the inside pocket of his well-tailored suit and pulled out an envelope. "Just this! If I didn't know Martha's handwriting, I'd say somebody was pulling a pretty lousy joke on me, and one in darned poor taste!"

He shoved the envelope, a squarish pink one, at me. I took it and plucked out the letter. It was short, and having known Martha all of her forty-seven years on this earth, I immediately recognized her neat, prim hand. It read, without salutation or signature, as follows:

The grave is fine, Charles, dear. Wish you were here.

I clamped the pipe between my teeth and laid the letter on my lap while I struck a match. I puffed a little blue cloud and picked up the letter again.

"It sure looks like her handwriting," I said. "How'd you get it?"

"Look at the envelope! Postmarked right here in Binsville yesterday! Came in the regular delivery today."

"In that case, Charlie," I said, giving the letter back to him, "I'd say you hit the nail on the head. Somebody is pulling a pretty lousy joke on you."

He shook his head vehemently. "That's her handwriting, Buzzy! I'd know it anywhere!"

"There are such things as forgeries. And there are people around this town who would go to pretty good lengths to put a fright into you."

"What do you mean by that?"

I leaned back and puffed on the pipe, then I turned and looked him squarely in the eye. "We've known each other ever since you came here about twenty years ago haven't we, Charlie?"

"It's twenty-five years, Buzzy, and yes, we have. Fact is, Martha and I didn't have a closer friend in Binsville than you."

"All right. So let's stop pussyfooting around. Some folks think you killed Martha."

"She was killed when the car ran off the road and hit that tree south of town!"

"Sure she was. That's exactly what the official death certificate said. Death by accident."

He stuffed the letter back into his pocket. "You were the first one to come along after the wreck. People trust you, Buzzy. You testified at the inquest that Martha was dead and I was unconscious. Why would anybody think I killed her?"

I reached over casually and took the corner of his jacket lapel and rubbed the rich material slowly between my thumb and forefinger. "How many men in this whole county can afford a suit like that? Two hundred and fifty if it cost a penny."

"Three hundred and a quarter," he said dully, slumping back in the rocker. "For her money, is that it?"

"In a nutshell."

He stood up suddenly, straight as a ramrod, jaws knotting. "That still don't satisfy me about the letter! I'm going to have a handwriting expert examine it!"

I saw Charlie again three days later. He had been up to Atlanta, he said, and from the looks of him he had doubled his intake of gin while maybe halving the vermouth. Charlie was one of those martini men. Very dry.

"Well?" I said.

He sighed. "I took all kinds of samples of her handwriting —checks, letters, grocery lists. Went to three different experts, and every one of them is ready to stake his reputation that Martha wrote that letter, no doubt about it."

Just about then old Mr. Grubb, the postman, came through my gate, stumbled around the empty cans and trash, and gave me the usual assortment of bills and occupant throwaways.

"Might as well save myself a trip up that driveway of yours, Mr. Adamson," he said to Charlie. "Here's a few things for you."

I had barely opened the bill from the Ace TV shop and glimpsed the blood-red stamp that read "LAST WARNING" and something about legal action, when Charlie let out a little squeak and dropped his mail to the porch floor.

"What's the matter?"

"It's—it's—"

Perspiration was popping out of his forehead like sap out of a skinned pine, and his eyes were sort of starting from the sockets. There was one letter still clutched in his hand, and I reached over and took it.

It was the same handwriting, on the same pink stationery.

> Charles Dear [Martha had called him that from the beginning],
>
> Please—please have some drain tile installed at the foot of the hill below the sycamore tree! With all this rain I have been positively afloat for the past week! The beautiful silk lining of the casket is all moldy and my blue organdy is absolutely ruined! Please, Charles dear, have this done without delay. Mr. Fenwick should give you a good price.
>
> Your,
> MARTHA

I got up and went into the house and brought out a half-empty bottle of vodka that had been in the cabinet for months. Charlie didn't even wait for me to go back for a glass.

I put Charlie Adamson in my bed that night and I slept on the couch. He had sent me on an urgent mission up the hill to his place for gin and vermouth after the vodka was gone, and by the time he had his fill of his favorite beverage, there was nothing left to do but drag him off to bed. I never could have gotten him up the hill by myself.

As I was tucking him in, I looked at his slack face and I could not help recalling the night of the wreck. He had looked the same then, except for a small streak of blood where his head had hit the steering wheel. It really hadn't been a bad wreck. Charlie couldn't have been going more than twenty or so when they hit that oil slick and whammed into the tree.

That was what got the talk started. Charlie had been little more than stunned, but Martha had received a massive skull fracture that killed her outright, apparently when she went forward into the dashboard. Folks with suspicious turns of mind whispered around that Charlie had set the whole thing up and killed her after purposely running the car into a tree.

Of course, there was no proof, but if it hadn't been for me, it might have looked pretty bad for him in a circumstantial way. Most of these same old folks could remember back when I was courting Martha. She was Martha Malone then, the only child of old man A. D. Malone, rest his soul, who owned something like half the land in the whole county. The good half.

Naturally, I was more than a little shaken up when Charlie Adamson came down from Atlanta on some kind of business with old man A. D., met Martha, and, within a month, married her. I had already made pretty detailed plans for my life as a country gentleman, bringing back the glory that once was the Busbys'.

Folks knew I had to be telling the truth when I said I saw the wreck happen, and when I got to the car Charlie was unconscious and Martha was dead.

After getting that second letter and drinking so much vodka and gin, Charlie declined the offer to join me for breakfast next morning. I sat there at my little table near the woodstove and had a big plate of grits and sidemeat and three eggs, sunny-side up and soft as baby oysters.

"Charlie," I said, stirring the eggs into the grits, "don't you think you ought to go to the police about this?"

He stumbled across from the bed to the sideboard where the gin bottle stood from the night before. He poured a hefty slug into a dirty glass, and without so much as uncorking the vermouth, turned it up. It seemed to steady him a bit after a few moments, and he came and sat down at the table.

"What would I tell them, Buzzy? That—that my dear departed wife is writing me letters from the cemetery?" He shook his head and poured another three fingers. "No thanks!"

Charlie went, like they say, from bad to worse after that. He drank night and day, and entirely stopped shaving or combing his hair. His three-hundred-and-twenty-five-dollar suit grew splotched and wrinkled, and anybody who didn't know him would have taken Charlie for a bum.

He came staggering down the hill almost every day to my place, bringing his bottle along with him. Whenever old Mr. Grubb happened by while he was there, Charlie would duck into the house and he wouldn't come out till the postman had delivered my mail and gone on.

It must have been about ten days after he got the letter about the drain tile. Charlie, as usual, was sitting in the rocker with a big dent in a bottle of gin. He didn't see old Grubb till he was standing right there in front of us.

"Well, hello there, Mr. Adamson," the postman said. He handed me Ace TV's positively and absolutely final notice and then with a little lick of his thumb he drew a pink envelope out of his bag and pushed it into Charlie's shaking hands. "Save me a trip up that driveway of yours."

Charlie just sat there for the next five minutes, staring open-mouthed at the letter. When I saw that's all he could do, I reached over and took it. It was another one from Martha, alright, and I read it to him. She thanked him for the drain tile (Charlie had called Mr. Fenwick about it the very next day after getting the letter) and went on to register a complaint about the worms. She asked him to check with Cal Lumpkin at the nursery about what might get rid of them. She went on to say how they tickled and she couldn't scratch.

That was the end of the line for Charlie Adamson. He left the gin bottle, empty, there on the porch and hightailed a crooked line up the hill. It wasn't more than two or three minutes before I heard the gun go off up there in the big house. It sounded to me like both barrels at once.

I sat there rocking slowly back and forth, and after a while I smiled. I never had been much for smiling, especially after Charlie and Martha went off on what I figured would be my honeymoon.

Just about everybody's got a weakness, I figure. Martha's was being a little on the peculiar side. Charlie's, if he had one, was dry martinis. I think mine was revenge. I started planning it fifteen years ago when I tossed that handful of rice after the newlyweds.

When they came back I acted like the same old Buzzy, and as the years went by both of them would come to me with their little problems. I was always a real good listener. I found that in between nods a good listener can get in a few licks of his own. So gradually, just a little at a time, I worked Martha around to believing that Charlie might try to kill her some day. After that, I kind of slipped her the idea of writing a series of letters from the grave, as it were, and letting me keep them. I promised her that if anything suspicious ever happened to her, and Charlie wasn't punished, I'd start mailing the letters. Martha wrote nearly sixty of them in all, fitted for dry weather, cold, hot, just about everything. Some were real corkers. I burned what was left after Charlie shot himself.

That finished the last half of my revenge. The night I found Charlie and Martha in the wreck, I had the first half of it. I killed Martha that night. I felt I ought to drag it out for my dear old pal Charlie.

Charlie has been dead a month now and is buried out there on the hillside next to Martha. That big shady old sycamore is over them. That should have been the end of it. But it wasn't. Old Mr. Grubb came by about fifteen minutes ago, and there, mixed in with the advertisements and bills, was a little pink envelope with a faint perfumey smell. There was a short, friendly note inside. It went like this:

> You naughty, naughty Buzzy-Wuzzy [Martha was the only one who ever called me that]. Who would have ever thought it of you! But Charles dear and I have agreed to be charitable and let bygones be bygones. We know you must be lonesome without us. The Busby plot is right next to the Malones', so you just hurry on out, and it'll be like old times. Just the three of us . . .
>
> MARTHA

I know I had a bottle of vodka around here someplace. I must invite old Mr. Grubb to share it with me.